The bell rang, and Sandy's hands tightened on the reins. She felt the chestnut mare give a small buck, and tensed with excitement.

"Come on then, Quest, let's go!"

With a new determination, girl and pony headed for the first jump, clearing it easily and heading across the arena at a fast canter. Quest sailed over the spread, leaped over the parallel bars, and soared over the imposing double before thundering down to the finishing line.

Sandy jumped down from the saddle and flung her arms around the chestnut pony's neck. "Clever girl, Questie. I think we've done it!"

Rowan morrison

Heronsway 1
Pony Quest

Elizabeth Wynne

An Armada Original

Pony Quest was first published in Armada in 1989

Armada is an imprint of the Children's Division,
part of the Collins Publishing Group,
8 Grafton Street, London W1X 3LA

Printed and bound in Great Britain by
William Collins Sons & Co. Ltd, Glasgow

"It's huge!"

Craning her neck, Sandy stood up on her cycle pedals and viewed the large, rectangular building which crouched low in the flat fields beside the road.

"That's only the indoor school," Tessa laughed from her bicycle. "Wait till we get to the motorway bridge."

With bent heads, the two girls cycled hard up the steep incline which took the lane over the motorway. When they reached the level, Tessa stopped her cycle and pointed towards the Equestrian Centre. "There! You can see it better now," she said.

"It's gigantic!" Sandy said, feeling that she was running out of appropriate words to describe this equestrian empire.

"It's not, you know," Tessa replied. "You should see the one at Ludleigh."

Sandy gazed at the two long rows of stables, at right angles to each other, overlooking a rectangular exercise area. There was a vast gravelled space, presumably for car parking, and beyond that were fields containing jumps of every description. To the right hand side lay the large, low building which Sandy had seen first, and which she now knew to be the indoor school.

"Well, it's gigantic compared to Crosslands," Sandy stated, with conviction.

"Is that where you used to ride, before you came to live here?"

"Mm. They had stables for eight ponies and Miss Middle's horse, Harry, a tack room-cum-office, and a barn for the hay and straw. And a field down the lane – that's all."

"Come on," said her new friend, remounting her bicycle, "Come and see Duskie – then I'll show you round."

Things were definitely looking up, Sandy thought to herself, as she followed Tessa down the slope from the motorway bridge. Today, even the shop hadn't looked too bad as she had swung in through the door, her school bag on her shoulder. There had been so much upheaval in her life recently, and the prospect of moving to a sweet shop with a tiny flat above had not held too much appeal a month ago, when her mother had decided on the move.

Sandy's mother had greeted her a little apprehensively, when Sandy entered the shop. "How was it?" she asked.

Sandy paused by the counter, where Mum waited for two children to make a protracted decision regarding chocolate bars.

"OK," she replied, lightly. "Well, great, actually," she added with enthusiasm.

Mrs Corfield looked relieved. She viewed her daughter across the two bent heads. "I put the kettle on," she began.

Sandy grinned. "I know, I know – the parent's

6

panting for her cuppa!" she said. "I'll do it," she added, pushing through the beaded curtains to the store-room.

This was the part of the shop that she liked the least. It was dim and shabby, with boxes and jars piled drearily from floor to ceiling, partly covering the small window at the back. Near the bead curtain was a small table, where all the necessities for tea-making were kept.

Sandy pressed the switch on the kettle and ladled tea into a sturdy brown teapot, while she thought of other things. Ponies! That was what she wanted to think about – not dreary old sweet shop store-rooms. She had been deprived of ponies for over a month, and she was beginning to feel desperate!

The tea made, Sandy filled two mugs, tucked the biscuit tin under her arm, and stepped back through the beads into the relative splendour of the shop. The two children had gone, and Mrs Corfield accepted the mug of tea gratefully. She sat on a stool and leaned back against the wall.

"Tell me about your day, then," Mum demanded, sipping her tea and looking at her 11-year-old daughter through the spiralling steam.

Sandy thought about it briefly. She had been dreading her first day at a new school. The last term of Junior School had not seemed the ideal time to move, but it had turned out to be a good day, after all.

"It was great," Sandy repeated. "I met this girl, you see, and she's got a pony, and—"

"Say no more," Mum interrupted, laughing.

Briefly, she turned her attention to a customer, who came in to pay for an evening paper which he had taken from a rack outside the door. "Where does she keep her pony?" Mum asked, when he had left.

"Well, that's it, Mum. She's calling for me at half past five and she's going to take me to see it. It's at an equestrian centre just outside town."

"Equestrian centre! Sounds a bit up-market!"

"That's what I thought. But Tessa says it's really good. The pony's stabled there, and Tessa looks after him herself. She cleans him out and feeds him twice a day. It's OK if I go, isn't it?"

"Where is this . . . this equestrian centre?"

"Off Pinn Road. Beyond the roundabout and down that lane. You remember – we saw all those lambs and wondered where the lane went?" Sandy studied her mother's face, anxiously. Mum had been so unsettled since the separation – she might even say no. For the hundredth time since Christmas, Sandy asked herself why they had done it. *Why* had her parents separated? But now was not the time to ask again. Mum was tired, and besides, Sandy wanted permission to be out late.

"What about homework?" her mother asked.

"Only a bit of reading," Sandy answered promptly, "and I did that at break, this afternoon."

"You're going on your bike, are you?"

Sandy nodded. A family burst in through the doorway, the mother bearing a paper and magazine from the rack, and three children clambering towards the sweet counter.

"All right," said Mrs Corfield, getting up from her stool to attend to her customers, "but no later than eight thirty."

"OK, Mum. Thanks. I'll get myself some cheese on toast, and wait for Tessa outside."

They had come to a large notice board announcing "Heronsway Equestrian Centre" and Tessa led the way carefully down a wide, cinder path which was liberally sprinkled with puddles and potholes.

"Sue and Peter can't afford to have this tarmacked yet," Tessa called over her shoulder, her voice jerking as she jolted her way between the holes, "the horseboxes have made a mess of the path."

"Are they the owners?" Sandy asked, when they stopped where the cinder path reached the gravelled car park area. Then, looking round, she added, "Where do they live?"

Tessa pointed to a corner at the side of the indoor school building. "In that caravan," she explained. "They can't afford a house yet, either!" she added.

"Are they nice?" Sandy asked, and her new friend answered with enthusiasm. "They're brilliant," Tessa said. "They've only been here about a year, you see, so things aren't quite finished yet. We'll just get rid of our bikes and then I'll take you to see Duskie," she added, her round face shining with pride.

Duskie recognized Tessa's call, and his black head appeared at the opening of stable number twenty-one. He whinnied his greeting, shaking his head up and down and tossing his long black mane impatiently.

"Oh, Tessa, he's gorgeous," Sandy said. "You *are* lucky."

"I know," Tessa admitted. "I'm not really used to it, myself. I've only had him for six months."

Tessa unbolted the lower door and the two girls let themselves into the stable. Contentedly, Sandy breathed in the smell of straw, hay and warm pony, patting Duskie's strong black neck, while Tessa chattered away about her pony.

"He's only six, and he's quite fizzy at times. He's thirteen three – just right for me because I'm small for my age and I can grow into him. He's got a lovely coat, hasn't he – it's a pity you have to clip them when they're in . . ."

Suddenly, Sandy felt a dig in her ribs.

"You're not listening to a word I'm saying," accused her friend.

"Sorry. I was. It's just that it's great to be back with ponies again," Sandy admitted.

"Well, I was going to say," said Tessa, beginning to unbuckle Duskie's day-rug, "that we've got time to go for a ride – and then I can show you round later on. Shall we?"

"You bet!"

"Here you are, then," said Tessa thrusting a dandy brush into Sandy's hand. "He doesn't need much – just his tail and that bit of muck on his near hind. I'll get the saddle and bridle."

It had been the best day of this year, so far, Sandy decided, as she lay in bed that night. She couldn't sleep. Ponies kept trotting through her mind – grey ponies, bay ponies, black ponies, chestnuts. There had been so many at the centre. Some had been tied outside their stables, watching while their owners worked at the straw with pitchfork and brush. Riders and ponies came and went all the time.

Sandy and Tessa had left by the cinder path, Tessa mounted on Duskie and Sandy riding her old bicycle. They had ridden along the lane beside a river, through countryside new to Sandy.

After about a mile, Tessa turned Duskie off the lane, across a bridge and on to a straight cinder path. Tessa explained that it was a track, one of many which went for miles across the moors, between the fields.

After a long, fast canter along the cinder path, Tessa handed Duskie over to Sandy and she, too, had cantered along the track. But, only too soon, it was time to return to the centre, as an evening mist rolled gently over the moors, leaving trees and hedges floating eerily over a soft white sea of mist.

"Going to be a fine day tomorrow," Tessa predicted, as she jogged along the lane on Duskie.

"How do you know?"

"Mist on the moors brings sunshine to your doors," she chanted in reply.

"Pity about school," Sandy commented.

"How about tomorrow morning?" Tessa asked, as she slid down from the saddle. Sandy looked puzzled. "I'll be here at a quarter to seven, as usual," Tessa explained. "I'll call round for you if you want to come."

11

"To muck out the stable, do you mean?"

"Yes," Tessa replied, "and fill the water bucket and the hay net and change Duskie's rug – there's plenty to do!"

"Great!"

Yes, it had been wonderful to be riding again, Sandy thought. But, lovely as Duskie had been to ride, it was another pony which remained in Sandy's mind as she drifted off to sleep. A chestnut pony about fourteen hands, with large, bright, interested eyes, and a dark forelock falling over a thin white blaze . . .

2

"I think I must still be dreaming!" Mrs Corfield propped herself up in bed and gazed wonderingly at her wide-awake, tray-bearing daughter.

"Just thought you'd like a cup of tea in bed to wake you up," said Sandy, innocently, "knowing your passion for cups of tea at all hours of day or night!" She put the tray down on the dressing table and carried a cup and saucer over to her mother's bedside table.

"A biscuit, too!" Mrs Corfield leaned back on her pillows and looked at her younger daughter with amused eyes. "What's the catch?" she asked, suspiciously. "I can't believe this is the daughter that I usually have to prise out of her bed on school mornings." She looked towards her alarm clock. "It's only twenty past six," she observed. "What's up today?" Her eyes were beginning to adjust to the light which streamed in through the gap where the bedroom curtains did not quite meet. "Aha!" she exclaimed. "You've got your jodhpurs on!"

"Is it OK, Mum?" Sandy asked hastily. "Tessa goes every morning, you see, to muck out the stable. I'll be back in time to put the papers out."

Mrs Corfield sipped at her tea. "You can go *every* morning if it means this luxury," she said. "I'll be able to finish typing out that article and have time for a proper bath this morning, before the shop opens." She leaned forward. "And *you'll* have to have a wash, too, Sandy. Leave yourself time. You can't go to school smelling of horses."

Sandy sighed. Really, Mum did fuss, sometimes. "OK," she agreed, "I'll even use that awful soap Aunt Cress sent me for Christmas, if you like."

As she pulled her bicycle out from the shed in the tiny courtyard at the back of the shop, Sandy heard the tap of the typewriter keys coming from the back bedroom. Mum must be getting on with her article. Sandy looked up and saw Boxer sitting on the window sill, his long tabby tail curled neatly round the fat, circular paws which had prompted his name. Boxer had settled in well to the small country town, having been a suburban cat all his life. Sandy let herself out of the yard and pushed her bike down the narrow alleyway which was shared with the two shops next door.

Boxer would be safe enough now, Sandy thought, for there was nothing busy about the main street at this time in the morning. The only vehicle in sight was a milk float, trundling slowly past the old clock tower which stood in the centre of the three joining roads at the end of the High Street.

A bicycle appeared, coming down the hill, and there was Tessa, waving cheerfully.

"I can't think which one you mean."

The two girls had stopped their cycles at the end of the cinder path.

"She's in that one," Sandy replied, pointing towards the further block of stables. "The second from the left, almost next to the tack room. Look – she's just put her head out!"

"Oh, *that* one," Tessa replied. "That's Quest." She wheeled her bicycle along to the side of the hay barn, where she propped it against the corrugated iron wall. "Quest belongs to Kay Carter," Tessa continued, "Kay works in the city and she doesn't really ride Quest enough."

"I think she's lovely."

The two girls made their way towards the nearest stables. Duskie looked out from one of the openings and whinnied.

"Hello, you lovely old thing," Tessa crooned, as she unbolted the door and let herself in. She talked to her pony as she fitted the headcollar and clipped on the lead rope. "We can put them out while we clean the stables," Tessa explained to Sandy. She led her pony out, and Sandy followed. Duskie snorted and tossed his head, prancing excitedly beside Tessa, as she led him towards the exercise area. She slid back the bar which served as a gate, and unclipped the lead rope. Duskie trotted off on the sawdust, snorting and high-stepping.

"Right! Let's get at it!" said Tessa.

As they passed by on their way to collect a wheelbarrow, Sandy paused by Quest's stable. The chestnut pony was looking out, watching the activity with interest.

"She's so lovely," Sandy said wistfully, stroking the pony's neck, while Quest pushed her nose hopefully against Sandy's anorak pocket. Sandy leaned over the stable door, studying the pony more closely. She was strongly built, and yet delicate at the same time, with a finely-chiselled head and beautiful, intelligent eyes. Sandy had always dreamed of owning a pony like this. "Don't you think she's lovely, Tess?" she said, turning to her friend.

"Ye-es," said Tessa, doubtfully.

"You don't sound very sure."

"Well," Tessa replied, "I do think she's lovely, but I've seen her in action when Kay rides her at the weekends. She's *really* fizzy. Goes bananas, sometimes!"

"Well, *I* think she's gorgeous," said Sandy emphatically. "I wish I could ride her."

"Come on," said Tessa, "we're never going to get that stable cleaned out."

The two girls worked with dedication, sorting through the straw with their pitchforks, tossing the good straw to the back of the stable and putting the droppings and soiled straw into the wheelbarrow.

"Makes a difference, having some help," Tessa observed. She leaned on her pitchfork. "We might even have time for ten minutes in the indoor school, if we put our skates on!" She grinned, ruefully,. "I daren't leave later than five to eight, though. Mum would go berserk!"

"Mine, too," Sandy agreed, changing to a broom and beginning to brush the floor. "I've got to be home by a quarter to eight. I always put the papers and magazines out for the shop, and we open at eight!"

Sandy brushed the last of the stable sweepings

16

on to the spade held by Tessa. This last spadeful duly deposited in the barrow, Tessa trundled off to the muck-heap at the back of the stable block. As Sandy hovered near the stable entrance, a tall girl passed by, wheeling a barrow. She smiled at Sandy.

"Hi!" she said, slowing her pace a little. "You a new recruit?"

"I'm with Tessa."

"Right. Well, I'm Chrissy. See you around." She hurried away at a brisk pace, whistling, and nearly collided with Tessa, who was on her way back, minus the wheelbarrow.

"Chrissy seems to be in a hurry," said Sandy.

Tessa laughed. "Chrissy's *always* in a hurry," she replied. "She's a working pupil. She looks after the livery horses and ponies – and Sue and Peter's own horses."

"Does she get paid?"

"Mm. A bit. It's not a lot – but it's more than the dole! And she says she's doing what she really *wants* to do. She works terribly hard." Tessa lowered her voice slightly. "Chrissy's got problems at home," she confided. "She told me about it. Her dad's unemployed – and pretty depressed about it. Chrissy works in the kitchen at a pub in the evenings to help with the bills. Her mother works too, but she's a bit . . . helpless, from what Chrissy told me. Chrissy's great, though," Tessa added, enthusiastically. "She works at the pub until after midnight – washing up, that sort of thing – but she's always here, mucking out, when I come at a quarter to seven. She's saving up to buy Merlin

17

from Sue, too," Tessa said, "but she says it'll take years.

"I'd like to be a working pupil when I leave school," Tessa told Sandy, as she led the way to the tack room, where saddles and bridles hung tidily on the walls. The owner's and horse's names were written on the wall above each set of saddlery. Hats, coats, buckets and rugs were propped or draped around the walls. It felt cosy, Sandy thought, seeing horsey posters on the walls and curtains at the two windows.

"How old is Chrissy?" Sandy asked.

"Dunno. About seventeen, I think," Tessa replied, lifting down Duskie's bridle. "There you are," she added, handing it to Sandy. "I'll bring the saddle."

"And why is she a pupil?" Sandy questioned, following Tessa along the concrete path towards Duskie's stable.

"Hey, Chrissy!" Tessa called to the older girl, who was coming back towards them, carrying half a bale of hay in her arms. "I'm being interrogated! Can you tell Sandy why you're a pupil. You've got exams, soon, haven't you?"

Chrissy stopped and put down her load. "That's right," she replied, pushing back her short dark hair. "I have three lessons a week, you see," she said, turning to Sandy. "One stable management and two riding or jumping. Hopefully, by the end of July, I'll be an A.I."

"What's that?"

"An Assistant Instructor. I've got to go away to Barrington Equestrian Centre for my exams."

18

"Written ones?"

Chrissy laughed. "No, thank goodness. They'll be practical and oral. I'll have a riding test, of course, and a jumping test and general horse management. I'll have to look smart and well turned-out, too – that will count in my marks."

"I hope you do well," said Sandy.

"Thanks," Chrissy replied, picking up the hay, "I'm determined to pass!"

"Sandy!" Tessa's head appeared in the opening of Duskie's stable. "Bridle! Come on – it's twenty past seven!"

The indoor school was a vast, purpose-built building. At one end, overlooking the schooling area, was raised wooden seating, and above that two windows looked over the school.

"What's up there?" Sandy asked as she followed Tessa and Duskie into the schooling area.

"Coffee bar!" Tessa called.

While Tessa began to put Duskie through his paces, Sandy leaned against the wooden fencing at the side of the schooling area, wondering what Miss Middle would think of Heronsway Equestrian Centre. At Crosslands, the nine stables had been draughty and antiquated, and the only place to escape to in bad weather had been the small shed which had served as an office for Miss Middle as well as a tack room. As she watched Tessa cantering Duskie in a figure of eight, Sandy remembered rainy days at Crosslands, when ponies and riders had returned from the ride soaked to the skin. The ponies had been rubbed down in their stables, but the riders who had remained to help had stayed damp all day, keeping warm by mucking out and carrying hay. Sandy noticed some signs over two doors at the far end of the indoor school. She grinned as she read "Ladies" and "Gentlemen", remembering trips behind the barn at Crosslands!

Warm breath on her face brought Sandy back to the present, and the salubrious surroundings of Heronsway. She looked up and found herself looking into Duskie's black face. He snorted excitedly, chewing on his pelham bit.

"Wakey, wakey!" Tessa called, leaning down from the saddle. "Do you want a go?"

"You bet!" Sandy replied. Then, looking at her watch, she added, "But I've only got five minutes."

"OK, Cinderella," Tessa said, cheerfully, jumping down and holding Duskie's reins while Sandy mounted.

As she trotted Duskie up one side of the dressage area, Sandy thought what a strange feeling it was to be riding on a sand-surface. She squeezed gently, and Duskie changed to a canter. Remembering her aids for cantering in a circle, Sandy concentrated on sitting well. Duskie was obviously used to dressage work. His head held high and his ears pricked, he cantered smoothly around the arena, moving collectedly.

Suddenly, Sandy's concentration was broken, as Duskie's stride faltered and he twisted violently sideways. Sandy pulled herself back into position in the saddle and regained her right stirrup, glaring up at the other rider who had entered the dressage area at a fast trot, straight into

Duskie's path. But for Duskie's evasive action, they would have collided.

The other girl, of about Sandy's own age, and riding a pretty skewbald pony of around fourteen hands, was already at the other end of the school, cantering her pony in a small circle, flapping her legs and leaning back in the saddle.

Seething, Sandy walked Duskie back to Tessa.

"Did you see that!" she exclaimed. Then, checking her watch again, she added quickly, "I'll have to go, Tess. I can't be late or Mum won't let me come in the morning again."

"Come on," said Tessa, turning to stare angrily at the girl on the skewbald, before walking beside Duskie towards the door.

"I've got to go, too," Tessa said. "That Andrea!" she added impatiently, "She's a menace!" They walked towards the stables, and Tessa nodded her head in the direction of the end stable. "Look! There's her mother, cleaning out the stable. Honestly, she's so spoilt, that girl . . ."

As they reached Duskie's stable, Sandy slid down. "Sorry I've got to rush," she said. "I'll just help you with the tack, and then I *must* go." Working quickly, Sandy pushed the irons up the leathers and raised the saddle flap to reach the buckles of the girth. These undone, she lifted the saddle from Duskie's back and rested it on the stable door. Tessa, who had removed Duskie's bridle, fitted the headcollar and tied her pony to a ring outside the stable. She picked up the saddle and bridle.

"See you at school, then," she said to Sandy. The two girls parted, Tessa making her way towards the tack room, while Sandy ran towards her bike.

Two minutes later, Tessa appeared at the tack-room door, her round face pink with excitement.

"Sandy! San-dy!"

Elegant equine heads turned, ears pricked with interest. Chrissy, pushing a loaded barrow past the hay barn, stopped in surprise. But all that could be seen of Sandy was a cloud of dust, as her bicycle bounced at a fast rate over the cinder path.

"Oh well," Tessa murmured to herself, "I suppose it can wait."

3

"Tessa Roberts!" Miss Daker's loud whisper was impatient. "*Do* sit still, *please*. You were late for Assembly – now, at least, try to stop fidgeting."

"It's Sandy, Miss Daker," Tessa hissed back. "She's outside. She's new, you see, and she doesn't know she can still come in. I kept her a place."

With a sigh, Miss Daker turned to look in the direction of Tessa's agitated gaze.

"Sandra Corfield, do you mean? Go on, then – let her in."

Wriggling past two others, Tessa scuttled back to the doors, behind which Sandy could be seen, hovering uncertainly. Pushing open the large glass doors, Tessa grabbed her friend's arm. "Quick!" she said, "They're still getting themselves together up front. I've saved you a seat."

The two girls managed to gain their seats just as Mr Maunder, the headmaster, began Assembly.

"Got something to tell you," Tessa whispered excitedly, keeping an eye on Miss Daker.

"What?"

"Sh. The eagle eye's on me again. Tell you after Assembly."

"I found it in the tack room after you'd gone."

The two girls were being swept along on the

flowing tide of pupils towards their classrooms. They were in different groups so there was little time to communicate before classes began.

Sandy looked puzzled. "What *are* you talking about, Tess?"

"One of the notices on the board. Look!" She thrust a piece of paper into Sandy's hand. "I copied it out for you. We could go out at lunchtime if you want to phone. See you at break." Tessa turned off into her classroom and was lost from sight.

In the classroom of 4B, Sandy sat at her desk and read Tessa's piece of paper.

'Responsible person required', it read, 'to help with the cleaning out, feeding and exercising of my pony during the week. Not weekends.' Then Sandy's heart lurched with excitement as she read on, 'Telephone Kay Carter, 529642, between 1 and 2 or after 6 o'clock.'

Quest needed someone to look after her! Excitement bubbled inside Sandy as she thought of the beautiful chestnut pony at the Equestrian Centre. Then she chewed her nails as she considered the possibility that some other ponyless person at the centre had seen the notice, and had already arranged things with Kay Carter.

Time moved slowly that morning. English, usually Sandy's favourite subject, was unbearably dull, as Mr Foster explained the form of the sonnet. Enthusiastically, he talked of iambic pentameter and rhyming couplets, while Sandy cantered Quest along the bridle paths of her mind. Then it was mid-morning break time, and an excited consultation with Tessa.

At lunchtime, the two girls slipped out of school to the public telephone box across the road. They squeezed in together, closing the door and shutting out the noise of the school playground. The slot accepted Sandy's 10p piece greedily, and she dialled the number. When Kay Carter answered, Sandy explained her reason for calling.

"I see – and how old are you, Sandy?" Kay's voice sounded friendly.

"I'll be twelve soon."

There was a pause, then Kay continued slowly, "Well, I *really* was hoping for someone a bit older. Quest's quite spirited, you see."

Sandy's hopes plummeted, but she persevered. "The pony I used to ride was quite strong, and had a mind of his own," she said, "but I could just clean her out and feed her, if you like," she continued, adding wistfully, "I think she's so lovely."

"Mm. Well, look, Sandy, shall we meet at the centre? Then we can talk properly. How about Saturday?"

So there was nothing to do now but wait for Saturday. Each morning and evening, during that long first week of term, Sandy visited the centre with Tessa. As soon as the girls had arrived and left their bicycles propped against the wall of the hay barn, Sandy would make her way to Number 8 stable to see Quest, with carrot and apple pieces in her anorak pocket.

Soon, Quest was waiting and watching for Sandy's arrival, when the chestnut pony would toss her beautiful head up and down, whinnying her greeting. Sandy longed more than ever to be able to ride her. Giving Quest her offerings, Sandy would then return to help Tessa muck out Duskie's stable.

By Saturday morning, Sandy was jittery with a mixture of excitement and pessimism. She had cleaned out Duskie's stable with Tessa, and Tessa had taken her pony to the indoor school. Sandy leaned against the door of Quest's stable and watched the object of her desire. Quest was pulling at a few pieces of hay which remained in her net. Then, seeing Sandy, she turned towards the door, pushing her soft nose against Sandy's arm.

"Kay usually comes at about 9 o'clock on Saturdays," Chrissy called out, as she hurried past with a loaded barrow. She grinned cheerfully at Sandy as she passed by. "Good luck," she said.

"Hello, Sandy!" Another voice called out, as Sandy turned back to stroke Quest again. Sue Venables arrived at Sandy's side, smiling warmly. Sandy had met Sue and her husband, Peter, during the week.

"I hear you're hoping to get the job of looking after Kay's pony," Sue said. Sandy nodded. Everyone seemed to know.

"Trouble is, Kay wants someone older," Sandy replied dolefully.

"Quest can be a bit of a handful," Sue admitted. "She just seems to have so much energy."

Sandy heard a car pull up on the gravel. "Ah, there's Kay now," said Sue, turning away from Quest and setting off towards the car park, her fair, shoulder-length hair bouncing purposefully, "I'll just go and have a word . . ."

Kay Carter was quite small and slight, with dark, very curly hair tied back in a pony tail. Sandy twisted her fingers nervously amongst Quest's long dark mane, while Sue talked to Kay for a few moments. Then Kay walked over to the stable, smiling. "Hello – you must be Sandy."

Sandy hadn't realized how nervous she was until she tried to reply, and heard an unintelligible squeak emitting from her own mouth. Clearing her throat, she tried again. "Yes. Hello," she replied huskily.

"I see you two have made friends already," said Kay. "Hello, old girl," she murmured to her pony, patting the shining chestnut neck and tickling Quest behind his ears. She unbolted the door and held it open for Sandy. "Come on in," she said, and Sandy followed her into the stable. Sandy had not been inside before. She patted Quest's strong shoulder, and the pony nudged her playfully. Certainly, Quest was a strongly built pony, Sandy thought. She seemed bigger, now that Sandy stood next to her. Her heart sank. Kay Carter would surely think that Sandy was too young to look after her pony.

Kay, who had moved to the other side of the pony, called out, "Could you pull her rug off, please, Sandy. I've unbuckled it."

Sandy slid the rug off, and folded it carefully.

"Thanks." Kay reappeared, ducking under Quest's neck. "Now, if you could take the rug to the tack room and leave it in my place – you'll see my name on the wall – and bring the grooming tools, we can give her a good grooming while we talk."

It wasn't until Kay Carter held Quest's reins and spoke to her, that Sandy began to hope.

"Up you go!" said Kay. "Let's just see how you get on in the exercise ring."

With a lurch of excitement, Sandy realized that Kay was about to judge her ability to ride Quest. Then, with a sudden realization, Sandy reminded herself that she had not yet actually *ridden* this pony she viewed with such adoration.

Tessa's words came back to her with a rush. "She's *really* fizzy," Tessa had said. "Goes bananas, sometimes!"

Sandy's confidence began to trickle away as she put her left foot in the stirrup, grasped the pommel, and propelled herself into the saddle. Sue's comment came back to her, too. She had told Sandy that Quest was a bit of a handful . . .

Sandy felt the energy and vitality beneath her and, as quickly as it had come, her nervousness vanished. At last she was riding Quest! As the pony danced excitedly on the spot, Sandy gathered up the reins, watching the small chestnut ears flicking back to listen for instruction, and seeing the pony's long mane shaking and falling in silken waves as Quest tossed her beautiful head.

Still holding the reins lightly, Kay moved off towards the exercise ring, with Quest dancing beside her. Delighting in the lightness of her mount's step, Sandy thought Quest felt as though she were taking part in a ballet for horses!

They reached the entrance to the practice area, and at last Sandy and Quest were alone. Concentrating on her riding position, Sandy held the excited pony on a light but firm rein. She squeezed tentatively with her legs, and Quest shot away like an arrow.

"Steady, girl, steady," Sandy murmured. She had forgotten Kay, the equestrian centre, everything. All she thought of now was riding Quest, and getting to know her.

Quest steadied to a canter. Sandy felt the energy that Sue had spoken of; Quest felt like a jack-in-the-box trapped under the lid and waiting to leap out once the box had been opened!

They neared the centre of the arena, cantering slowly and neatly round in a tight circle.

"Nice circling," Kay commented from the fence. Sandy relaxed and smiled across at Kay. Then Quest sprang from her jack-in-the-box with an enormous and joyous buck. Barely had the smile faded from her lips, than Sandy found herself sitting in the sawdust, with Quest bucking and dancing away from her!

For a moment, Sandy almost *hated* those strong chestnut hindquarters, as they careered across the sawdust. Quest had ruined her chances! Then the pony turned and stopped. She stood, snorting excitedly, tossing her head and shaking the reins, which hung loosely about her neck. She looked very pleased with herself – and very beautiful, Sandy thought, her devoted feelings returning.

Sandy scrambled to her feet. Without daring to look at Kay, she walked over to Quest, grasped the reins and jumped quickly back into the saddle. A tender rage was inside her. She adored this beautiful, headstrong, time bomb of a pony. She had wanted *so* much to look after her and ride her – how *could* she have spoiled everything like this?

With a new determination, which ran down the reins and made itself known to Quest, Sandy set off again. This time, the circle was completed without a hitch. When Sandy halted the chestnut mare in front of her owner, she knew that at least she had gone down fighting! Quest had obviously spoiled everything, but at least Sandy had finished in control. Quest stood quietly now.

Sandy was amazed to see that Kay was smiling broadly.

"Well done!" she said.

"But ... I made a complete mess of it!" Sandy admitted.

Kay Carter ducked beneath the fencing and came over to pat her pony. She held the reins while Sandy dismounted. "She can be a little vixen at times," Kay said, "but you showed her who's boss. Sue told me that you could handle a pony well – she's seen you riding Duskie in the indoor school – but I wanted to see for myself." Kay checked the girth before jumping lightly into the saddle. "I'm off for a ride, now," she told Sandy. "We'll have a proper talk when I come back, shall we?" She and Quest began to move away towards the edge of the practice area. "I'll be very pleased, Sandy," she called back, "if you'll look after Quest for me during the week, in return for riding. Is that all right with you?"

4

"It's no good. You can't get any sense out of her."
Tessa leaned forward in Duskie's saddle and spoke
to Sarah in a mock whisper, loud enough for Sandy
to hear. "She's been like this all morning – ever
since she heard that she can look after Quest."

Sandy emerged from her daydream. "Idiot!" she
said, grinning at Tessa. "What have I done?"

"Just ignored a perfectly good offer of a ride
on a really *good* pony – that's all!"

"Oh . . . I . . ." Sandy looked puzzled and Sarah
rescued her.

"I just wondered if you'd like to try Puffin,"
Sarah offered shyly. She was a quiet girl, rather
timid in her approach to other people – and to
her riding. Puffin had been presented to an over-
joyed Sarah on her thirteenth birthday, about two
months earlier, and the two of them were still getting to know each other. Sarah was small and slight
for her age, pale-faced and tense, with an anxiety
which showed in her riding. However, Puffin, a
finely built dapple-grey pony of just over fourteen
hands – "the best money could buy!" as Sarah's
rather overbearing father had pointed out on more
than one occasion – had a calm and well-mannered
disposition, and Sarah's confidence was growing
slowly.

"You'll have to be quick," Tessa pointed out. "Sue will be starting lessons again soon."

Sarah's pale face flushed as she said eagerly, "Yes – I'm having a jumping lesson at twelve-thirty."

"I'm getting used to very quick and exciting rides," Sandy admitted, grinning wryly at Tessa. Turning to Sarah, she added hesitantly, "I'd love to ride Puffin . . . if you're sure . . ."

Sarah slipped down from the saddle and handed Sandy the reins. "Really – I'd like to see how Puffin goes with you." She looked down at the ground as she added, "I – I'm really not very good with Puffin yet. I love him, but . . ."

Sandy stroked Puffin's smooth neck. "No – you look OK, honestly," she told Sarah earnestly. "You just . . . lean forward too much, I think." She gathered up the reins and mounted the grey pony, who stood quietly. Sandy squeezed gently with her legs, and Puffin moved off smoothly towards the main dressage area, where Tessa was practising a working trot on Duskie.

Sandy and Puffin followed Duskie across the school. Sandy urged her mount into a trot. But it wasn't as though he needed *urging*, Sandy thought. She had never before ridden a pony quite like Puffin. It was as if he knew, instinctively, what was required of him. Obviously, he had been expertly schooled to a high standard. Sandy eased him back to a walk as they followed Duskie down one length of the arena.

Puffin held his head beautifully, and his neat trot was smooth and comfortable. At the end of the arena, they turned; halfway along the next length,

Sandy gave the aids for a canter. She could hardly believe the smoothness of his gait and the neatness and precision with which he took her round in a wide circle. He did not turn his head to left or right, but his whole body curved slightly in the direction of the circle, as he cantered effortlessly, snorting gently with pleasure at each stride.

Out of the corner of her eye, Sandy saw Sue Venables enter the indoor school and she knew that it must be time for Sarah's lesson. She reined in, and Puffin came to a halt.

"Good boy. That was lovely." Sandy patted the grey pony and walked him over to the fencing where Sarah waited.

"He's fantastic to ride," Sandy enthused, sliding down from the saddle and handing the reins over to Sarah. "So well-schooled. I didn't know ponies could *be* like that!"

Sarah turned pink with pride. "He's such a *kind* pony, too," she said. "I don't think he'd ever think of doing anything remotely *vicious*."

"Puffin the paragon!" said a voice, laughing, and Sue appeared beside them. She held the reins while Sarah mounted. "Seriously though, Sarah," she continued, "Your father was very lucky when he went out and bought Puffin. So often when people who know very little about horses go out with money in their pockets, they get sold a pup! You've got to be so careful. It's best to take some-one really knowledgeable with you when you go out searching for a pony." She smoothed Puffin's grey neck, reflectively. "But your dad bought a real corker!" she added. "And he's turning out to be a very useful little jumper, too. Come on, Sarah, let's see how we get on today."

Sandy and Tessa stood outside the fencing, watching Sarah's lesson in progress. Duskie rested one hind leg and dozed, his black head leaning against Tessa's arm. Outside, rain was lashing down from a leaden grey sky, and the indoor school seemed the best place to be, just now.

Sue had set up three jumps for Sarah and Puffin to tackle. They were all about a foot in height, but were of varying types. One was a brush fence, the second a wall, and the third was a spread of three poles. Puffin could tackle these obstacles easily. The problem for Sue was to help Sarah have the confidence to ride her pony so that he took off from the correct place for each jump.

As the two girls watched, they were joined by Adam, another regular visitor to the centre. He trotted into the indoor school on Jasper, a strong dark bay pony belonging to the centre. Adam, who was just twelve, came regularly to Heronsway, but did not own his own pony. He had a lesson twice a week, and came at other times to help out generally.

"Hi!" said Tessa, cheerfully. "Have you got a lesson after Sarah?"

Adam shook his head. "Not really," he admitted. "I've had my two lessons this week." He leaned forward from Jasper's saddle, and his brown eyes looked puzzled. "Actually, Sue was being a bit mysterious," he confided to the two girls, who listened with interest. Jasper chewed on his bit, restlessly, excited at the prospect of some jumping.

"How do you mean, mysterious?" asked Tessa.

"Well, I'd mucked out Jasper's stable while he was out on a ride," Adam explained, "and then when he came back, I groomed him. He didn't really *need* grooming. I just like him, you see."

"And?"

"Well, Sue came by and said she wanted to see me in the indoor school – with Jasper. She said I could saddle up, and come in to here for an extra jumping lesson, if I liked – for free!"

"Can't be bad," commented Tessa.

"That's what *I* thought," agreed Adam, "but *why*? What's up, I wonder? She seemed to be excited about something."

"You'll soon see," Sandy pointed out. "She's finished Sarah's lesson," she continued, nodding her head in the direction of the main arena. "She's coming over."

"Oh good, you're here, Adam." Sue Venables looked round at them all. "I'm glad you're here, too, Tessa – and this might interest you as well, Sandy."

The four looked at each other blankly and then anxiously back towards Sue, who laughed as she commented, "You look like four naughty children who've been caught out doing something they shouldn't!" Then she pulled a letter from her back pocket.

"Now listen," she said, excitedly, "I've had a challenge from Lollington Stacey—"

"That's the equestrian centre beyond Cridge-leigh, isn't it?" Tessa queried.

"That's it," Sue replied, "and they have challenged us to a three-day event for a team of six riders," she continued, "A local tack shop near them has offered a challenge cup and sponsorship."

"Sounds great," said Tessa. "where will it be held – at Lollington Stacey?"

"Well, yes – and no," Sue replied. "You see, it won't take place all at once. Their idea is to spread it out over four weeks. They want the first event – the dressage – to take place here, even though their indoor school is bigger than ours."

Sandy gazed round her, trying to visualize anything bigger than this vast building. Her attention returned to Sue as she heard her say "and they will hold the cross-country there, at Lollington Stacey, since they have a particularly good course." Sue beamed round at them all. "Isn't it a great idea?" she said.

"What about the jumping?" Sandy asked.

"She was day dreaming again!" Tessa told Sue, with a grin. Turning to Sandy, she explained, "They don't know where the jumping will be yet, but they're asking Ludleigh Equestrian Centre if they can hold it. Sounds great," Tessa repeated, turning back to Sue. Although the youngest of the four, Tessa was generally their spokesman. "Who will you choose for the team?" she asked.

Sandy became aware of another pony entering the indoor school. She turned to see Andrea riding her pony towards them.

"Well you see," Sue explained, looking round at them, "Lollington Stacey are organizing this event to encourage the younger riders, so out of the six members of the team, at least three must be under fourteen, and all the ponies must be fourteen two or under."

"*My* pony's only fourteen one," came a voice. They all turned to look. Andrea was looking down from her pony's saddle.

"I've chosen my team already, Andrea," Sue told her, adding diplomatically, "You and Ragamuffin are coming on quite well – but you really *must* listen to what I tell you about your riding. You're not going to get the best out of your pony until you learn to sit properly and use your legs correctly."

Andrea turned red. "Well, who *is* in your team, then?" she demanded, sulkily.

Sue, addressing the others, said, "I've spoken to Chrissy and she'll ride Merlin. Kay Carter will ride Quest, and I'll ride Beauty." She looked round at them all as she continued. "That leaves the under fourteens. Tessa – how about you and Duskie?"

Tessa's freckled face shone with pleasure. "Me and Duskie!" she repeated incredulously. "You bet!"

"And Adam, what about you? I thought you could ride Jasper. He's very dependable and he's a great little jumper." She grinned as she added, "and *your* jumping has come on leaps and bounds – if you'll pardon the pun!"

"Terrific!" Adam looked surprised and pleased.

Sue turned her attention to Sarah. "And would you like to be a team member, Sarah?" she asked.

Sarah, who had returned enthusiastically from

her jumping lesson, now looked anxious. "Oh . . . I don't know . . ." she stammered.

"I'm sure you can do it, Sarah," Sue urged. "You know how competent Puffin is. He'll be a real asset to our team—"

"But I don't think I—"

"Yes, you can," Sue broke in, firmly. "You must give yourself a chance. At least have a try. Let Puffin teach you."

"Well . . . all right, I'll try." A small light of determination shone in Sarah's eyes.

"Good. That's settled, then." Sue smiled round at them all. "Now, all we need is lots of practice."

"When will the dressage be?" asked Adam.

"May the twelfth – less than a month," Sue replied. "We've got a lot to do. I'll let you all have a copy of the dressage course, so that you can practise. And next week, we'll meet up again to see how we're getting on. Ah – hello, Kay! I've just finished telling them about the competition."

"I'm looking forward to it," said Kay. She smoothed Quest's neck affectionately. "And *you*'d better behave yourself," she told the chestnut pony fondly.

"See you all here next week," said Sue. "I'll be with you in a moment, Adam," she added.

As she walked towards the office, Sue saw Andrea, a sulky scowl on her face, flapping her way around the dressage area on her pony, Ragamuffin.

"That Andrea!" Sue exclaimed to her husband. She banged about the office angrily.

"What's she doing?" asked Peter Venables mildly.

"Just being her usual spoilt self," Sue replied

tartly. "I can't seem to make her understand that she needs to improve her riding – to *think* about what she's doing. She's going to ruin that pony of hers, if she's not careful. I wonder if I ought to say something to her mother."

"That wouldn't do any good," her husband pointed out. "You know what her mother's like about Andrea – thinks she's the most wonderful thing since sliced bread!"

Sue laughed. "Oh well," she said, sighing, "Perhaps someone will make her see sense, one day . . ."

In Quest's stable, Sandy had made her arrangements with Kay Carter. Kay had left, and Sandy was hanging over the stable door, having a last, lingering look at the chestnut pony before she, too, left the centre. She always helped her mother at the shop on Saturday afternoons.

"You're the loveliest pony in the world," Sandy told the chestnut mare. Quest turned her intelligent brown eyes in Sandy's direction, munching reflectively at her hay. She snorted companionably and then pulled at some more hay, tossing her head impatiently.

"I'm glad you and Kay are in the team," Sandy continued, "but I wish . . ." There she stopped. It was no good to wish too much. She had had her most important wish granted. She was going to be able to ride Quest during the week, and look after her. That was enough for now.

Soon, Quest was left to her hay-munching, as Sandy's bike bounced away from Heronsway, down the cinder path to the rain-washed lane.

Mum's slight lack of enthusiasm was not noticed straight away by Sandy. As they sat together over the evening meal, after the shop was shut, Sandy chattered non-stop.

"She's such a gorgeous pony, Mum. You'll have to come and see her. She's chestnut with a white blaze, and she's got a lovely face – kind of wicked and intelligent at the same time, but really gorgeous. I think she might have some Arab in her . . ."

"I will come sometime," Mrs Corfield promised, "Perhaps one Sunday afternoon . . ."

"Mm. Well, of course, Kay might be out on her then."

"I don't have much time, that's the trouble, with the shop . . ." Mrs Corfield paused. "Sandy?"

Sandy looked up from stroking Boxer. There was a note in Mum's voice which demanded attention.

"Yes?"

"Sandy, we must talk a bit, mustn't we? I mean, it's only the two of us, with Julie away at college, and now that Dad's not here—"

Sandy opened her mouth to speak. Perhaps now was her chance to ask about the separation.

"I want you to go on doing things you enjoy, like riding," Mum continued, "but I'm very busy with the shop and . . . I rely on you to be sensible about it—"

"What do you mean, Mum? Do you mean you and—"

"I can't be in the shop *and* making sure that

you do your homework," Mum interrupted. "It sounds to me as if you're going to spend quite a lot of time at the centre – you won't let your school work suffer, will you?"

Later on that evening, Sandy lay spreadeagled on her bed, trying to puzzle it all out. Her school books were scattered about her, but Sandy's thoughts were concerned with her parents' separation. Why wouldn't Mum talk about it? Every time Sandy tried to broach the subject, Mum found something else to discuss.

"Really, Boxer," Sandy told the sleepy cat, "I don't understand parents." She tickled his chin, where his fur was soft and a pale creamy-brown. A thought began creeping into Sandy's mind. Perhaps Mum wanted to be back with Dad again? That must be it – *that* was why Mum didn't seem to want to talk about it! So, Sandy thought, smoothing Boxer's tabby fur and feeling a purr rumble through his body, she must do something about it. She must try to get them together again!

The parent problem temporarily shelved, Sandy's thoughts reverted to their favourite topic – ponies; in particular, Quest. She wouldn't see Quest tomorrow, since she would be spending most of the day with Dad. Perhaps Kay would be practising the dressage course. Sandy leaned back against her headboard and conjured up Quest in her mind – beautiful Quest, trotting and cantering round the dressage area in the indoor school. Then excitement twisted inside her as she remembered that next week *she* would be able to ride the pony that she adored so much. Living at Clereton was proving to be bearable after all!

5

"That's better, Tessa. Much more rhythm. Duskie looks more relaxed. Don't let yourself get stiff, either." Sue Venables stood in the middle of the indoor school, while Tessa rode Duskie over the dressage course. It was Monday, the markers were in place, and Tessa was attempting the course for the first time.

"Keep it going," Sue called, "Nice and relaxed. Down the centre line to C."

Tess shrieked suddenly. "Which way? I can't remember!"

"Left!" called Sandy from the fence. "Then circle left from E."

"Thanks," muttered Tessa, as she passed by at a working trot. Having completed the circle, she passed by again, trotting on to the marker K, where she urged Duskie into a canter.

"Steady, Tessa," Sue instructed from the centre. "Don't forget – nice and relaxed. It's just a working canter you want – it's not a race!"

With the aid of some further prompting from Sandy, and from Adam, who was also watching, Tessa completed the course, halting at G and saluting to imaginary judges, while Duskie stood quietly.

"Good. Nice halt," said Sue. "Remember not to let him step back – that's most important."

With a loose rein, Tessa walked Duskie over to Sue, who had joined the others by the fencing.

"Can I do it again, Sue?" Tessa asked, "I keep forgetting the course."

"Yes, *you* can do it again – but not on Duskie!"

Tessa looked blank, so Sue explained. "One of the main objects, Tessa, is to have a calm, relaxed pony, obedient to the aids of his rider." She patted Duskie's shoulder. "If you overtax him, he might become bored, and a bored pony isn't relaxed and obedient!"

"So who *can* I do it again on?" asked a puzzled Tessa.

"On shanks's pony," Sue replied.

Tessa still looked mystified. Sue laughed. "Your own two feet!" she explained. "That's the best way to learn the course. You can practise the different movements on Duskie – some of them when you're out on a ride. That makes it all much more interesting for him – and for you.

"The other way to learn the course," Sue said, as they all walked towards the exit, "is with a plan and a stick in the tack room." She turned to look at them all. "Whatever you do, don't bore your ponies. We can't expect miracles. We'll do the best we can and hope that, on the day, we and the ponies enjoy ourselves!"

"Sue's right, I suppose," Tessa said, as she and Sandy walked back towards the stables. She looked down at Sandy from Duskie's saddle. "Is Quest ready?" she asked.

"Polished and shining!" Sandy informed her.

"I've just got to saddle up and we'll be there!"

Sandy's fingers were trembling with excitement as she buckled the throatlash and tucked in the leather end. She pulled Quest's long forelock from under the headband. Then, unbolting the door, she led Quest proudly out into the yard area. She re-bolted the door and quickly checked the stable. No brushes lying about and the headcollar was hanging neatly. Then, with a light leap, she was in the saddle at last!

Quest was excited, too. She had been in the stable all day, and now she danced on the spot and tossed her head.

"Come on!" said Tessa, moving away towards the drive. "Quest looks as if she's about to burst!"

"It's great!" said Sandy, unable to stop the grin which seemed to have taken over her face.

"You look as if you've just been told that school's been abolished!" said Tessa.

"Well, this is the best thing that's *ever* happened to me," Sandy stated, emphatically. "I know it's not like having my own pony, but to be able to—"

But Sandy's euphoric mood was quickly dispelled. As Quest gave one of her enormous and enthusiastic bucks, Sandy found herself thrown forward onto the pony's neck. Awkwardly, she scrambled back into the saddle, accompanied by shrieks of laughter from Tessa.

"She's a menace!" Tessa declared, when she had recovered.

"No, she's not!" Sandy countered, protectively. "She's just . . . eager to go and full of life!"

"Well, I hope Duskie wasn't watching. He might

get some wrong ideas! Come on," she added, "let's get some of that energy out of her."

Tessa led the way down the cinder path at a brisk trot. Quest followed with a high and bouncy gait, snorting noisily.

All the way down the lane, Quest pranced and snorted. She jumped at every rustle – real or imaginary. When the ponies came to a field of young bullocks, Quest halted and stood as if turned to stone, her head thrown up high. Her nostrils were distended and she emitted a loud and long snort.

"She's going to breathe fire any minute!" Tessa exclaimed. "Watch out!"

But, having studied the bullocks for a few minutes, Quest was persuaded to move on. This time, she moved more naturally, and Sandy enjoyed the chestnut pony's smooth, long-striding trot. They trotted down the lane until they reached the track.

Tessa turned in the saddle and cast a quizzical look in Sandy's direction. "Canter?" she asked.

"Yes," Sandy replied, "but perhaps I should go first."

"Mm. I agree. Don't fancy that thunderbolt charging up behind me," Tessa commented, moving aside to allow them to pass.

Sandy squeezed gently with her legs, and Quest became the thunderbolt which Tessa had predicted. She shot away at a fast canter which quickly became a gallop. "Better let her get it out of her system," Sandy told herself, leaning forward and keeping a firm contact with Quest's bit. Hedges, ditches and trees flashed past, while

46

Sandy reminded herself that she had never been so fast on a pony before. But the cinder surface was firm, and the track was straight, so Sandy leaned forward a little more in the saddle, exhilarating in the strength of Quest's gallop and feeling the pony's long chestnut mane against her face.

The end of this stretch of track was in sight, where the path turned at right angles to both left and right. Sandy eased on the reins, and she felt Quest respond. Soon, they were travelling at a sharp canter. Sandy eased again and Quest slowed to a trot. At the end of the track they halted, and Sandy turned in the saddle.

In the distance, little Duskie was cantering fast, his long black mane bouncing against his neck.

"Good girl," Sandy murmured, patting the chestnut pony's warm neck. A feeling of joy surged over her as Quest flicked back an ear to listen. They were getting to know each other already! She was really very well-mannered, Sandy thought, as Quest stood quietly, her head turned to watch the approach of Tessa and Duskie.

"What kept you!" Sandy called out, as they came within earshot. Tessa and Duskie slowed to a trot, and Tessa patted her pony's neck.

"We didn't know we were coming out with a racehorse!" Tessa commented, as they stopped beside Quest. "How does she feel?"

"Gorgeous! I've never ridden a pony like Quest before!"

"I'm not surprised! They've all been on the race-track! I think she'd be too much of a handful for me," Tessa admitted. She patted her pony's neck again. "We like the quiet life, don't we, Duskie?" she said. Then, looking down the next track, which stretched ahead into the distance, she added, "Let's practise the straight bits of dressage – like Sue said."

"Good idea," Sandy said. "We can practise working trot, followed by a halt and then straight off into a working trot again – that's right at the beginning of the course."

A somewhat wet April gave way to May sunshine. On the Friday evening before the bank holiday weekend, Sandy was surprised to receive a telephone call from Kay Carter.

"Can you do me a favour, Sandy?" Kay asked. "Could you look after Quest for me this weekend – and ride her if you want to?"

"You bet I could!"

"Oh, good. Perhaps you could practise some of the dressage? We've been asked to a friend's house for the holiday, you see, right at the last moment . . ."

Hardly able to believe her good fortune, Sandy spent all her spare time at the equestrian centre over the bank holiday. She and Tessa went for a long ride on the Sunday, across the moors, over the main road and up into the hills, where they were able to canter for miles through wide, fern-sided paths. They took their lunch with them, tied behind the saddles, and stopped near a brook, where the ponies could drink. They returned on Sunday evening with two tired ponies and two sun-reddened faces.

On Monday afternoon, Sue organized a dressage

practice. She had gathered all the team members together, except for Kay. Sandy sat astride Quest, next to the barrier fencing, to watch the proceedings.

A pony entered the indoor school through the huge, sliding door, and Sandy was surprised to see that it was Ragamuffin, ridden by Andrea. Looking at Andrea's discontented face, Sandy wondered, with sudden insight, whether Andrea was lonely. Tessa had said that she was an only child, adored and spoiled by her parents. Sandy knew the lonely feeling of being an only child, even though she wasn't one. Julie, her sister, was eight years older, and had never wanted to play with her kid sister. Now, Julie was away at college and hardly ever came home.

Deciding to forget Andrea's previous behaviour, Sandy made an effort at friendliness.

"Hello," she said, smiling, "have you come to watch?"

Andrea glowered at her. "No – I was going to do some dressage," she stated coolly, "but the school seems to be full." Then, sensing that Sandy was trying to be friendly, and might be persuaded to be an ally, she leaned over towards her and added, "*I* think it was really *mean* of Sue not to choose me for the team."

"She didn't choose me, either," Sandy pointed out.

"But *you* haven't got a pony of your own," Andrea said, tactlessly, "and *I've* been here for *ages* – much longer than *them*."

"Well, Sue did explain about your riding," said

Sandy, exasperated. "Why don't you stay and watch with me – we'll probably learn a lot."

But Andrea just yanked her pony's mouth as she turned him away, kicking Ragamuffin's sides clumsily and hard.

"Poor Ragamuffin," thought Sandy. "He looks a good pony. He must have a good temperament, too, to put up with that sort of treatment."

The practice was a disaster! Sue on Beauty and Chrissy on Merlin completed the course without any particular mishap but when it came to Tessa's turn, she and Duskie seemed doomed to failure. Everything went wrong and they completed the course only with much prompting from the onlookers.

"I'm hopeless!" wailed Tessa, as she finished. "What*ever* am I doing?"

"Don't worry," Sue said, soothingly. "It's just nerves. You'll be all right on the day. But Tessa," she added, "*do* try practising the course on your own, without Duskie. Do it right through, several times – all the circling, everything. But don't worry," she repeated, smiling, "I think Duskie's just tired from his long ride yesterday."

Sarah was next to go. She sat tensely in the saddle while Puffin took her sedately around the dressage course until suddenly Puffin and Sarah parted company! One moment Puffin was cantering smoothly around the arena and the next, as he turned to commence the circle, he was riderless.

Sarah rose sheepishly from the sawdust, brushing off her jodhpurs, and holding up a stirrup leather and iron. "Sorry!" she called, "it came off. Can't have been on properly."

"Never mind," consoled Sue, "At least it has happened at a practice, Sarah," she continued. "You wouldn't have been very happy if it had happened next week, would you?"

Next week! Sarah, Tessa and Adam looked at each other as the awful truth dawned. The dressage competition was approaching fast. Suddenly, it didn't seem like such a good idea!

Sue walked over. "Another thing, Sarah," she said, quietly, "is that, really, you shouldn't have fallen off. You must have been pressing down on the stirrup iron instead of using your seat and your legs for staying in place." Sarah flushed. "It's all right," Sue added, hastily. "We can remedy it. Lots of riding without stirrups – that's what you need."

"I'll do that," agreed Sarah earnestly. She patted Puffin enthusiastically as she added: "At least I've fallen off, at last!"

"Goodness! Haven't you fallen off before?" asked Sue.

Sarah shook her head. "And it wasn't as bad as I thought," she admitted. She turned back to Sue. "Puffin was good, wasn't he?" she said, her eyes shining with pride, "apart from me falling off, I mean."

"I think you and Puffin are going to be a very good team, soon," Sue said quietly.

"Come on, Adam," she called out, "There's nothing else that can go wrong now. Let's see how you and Jasper get on."

For two minutes, all went well. Then Jasper stopped, halfway down one side of the dressage area. Adam, going red in the face, urged him on, but Jasper just put his ears back disdainfully, planted his feet firmly in the sawdust, and relieved himself!

The onlookers collapsed into a state of hilarity, and Sue declared the dressage practice at an end.

"I don't think it's quite our day, today," she observed, wryly. "I'm off to have a coffee. Anyone else coming?"

That evening, as Sandy and Tessa cycled home through the dusk-filled lanes, they hardly spoke. Tessa's mind was walking and trotting up, down, across and round the dressage arena, and cantering in beautiful, controlled circles. Sandy's thoughts were, as ever, of Quest. She was convinced that Quest's sometimes unpredictable behaviour was due to pent-up energy. Quest had been much calmer and quieter to ride over the holiday weekend, and Sandy thought that this was probably because she had had a lot of exercise. Still, Sandy had to admit that the chestnut mare was a lively ride . . .

Sandy broke the silence. "I'm glad, in a way, that I'm not riding in the competition," she observed.

"Mm. Don't blame you," Tessa replied. "Tell you what," she added, grinning sideways at Sandy across the handlebars. "After today's practice, you can ride Duskie, if you like, and I'll drop out!"

"No thanks," Sandy replied, wickedly. "I'll just stand at the side and laugh!"

At this point, their leisurely ride home became a race, as Tessa chased her mocking friend home, accompanied by much laughter.

6

It was on Monday of the following week – just six days before the dressage competition – that Sue broke the news.

All week, the younger members of the team practised, taking care to follow Sue's advice about not boring their ponies. Sarah rode Puffin everywhere without stirrups. The leathers and irons were crossed over, out of the way, in front of the saddle. Soon, the improvement in her riding was noticeable.

"What's happened to Sarah?" Kay asked, on Saturday morning, as she leaned over Quest's stable door to speak to Sandy. Sandy was never far from Quest's stable, even at weekends, when Kay took over the mucking out and feeding routine.

"I've got a feeling," Sandy replied, watching Sarah and Puffin trotting round the exercise area, "that it was falling off that did it – gave her more confidence."

"But she only slipped off, didn't she, when her stirrup parted company with the saddle? That's what Sue said."

"Yes, but . . ." Sandy leaned forward, confidentially. "She told us about it afterwards. She hadn't *ever* fallen off before, you see – and she was really nervous about it. Then she found it wasn't so terrible after all. And all that practising without stirrups has helped. I've been trying it, too, on Quest."

"She looks *so* much better in the saddle," Kay said, still watching Sarah, "And Puffin's such a dear – so reliable." She turned to pat Quest, who had pushed her nose over the door, inquisitively, "Not like *you*, you scoundrel!"

"Oh, but she's much better – I'm sure!" Sandy quickly jumped to the chestnut pony's defence, and Kay laughed.

"I was only joking!" she said. "I love her, too, you know!"

A moment later, she added, "I think I'll have a short rest," let herself out of the stable. She sat down on a bale of straw. "Tell me all about Quest's improvement," Kay said.

Leaning against the stable door, with Quest munching meditatively by her shoulder, Sandy told Kay how Quest's behaviour had altered with more exercise. Kay listened, nodding appreciatively.

"Yes," she agreed, "I don't have time to ride her enough, really. She's young – and full of spirit." She smiled up at Sandy. "In fact, we've got a very good arrangement, haven't we?" she added.

"A wonderful arrangement!" agreed Sandy, en-thusiastically. Then she added, "I'll muck out the stable now, if you're tired."

"Oh, Sandy, *would* you? To tell you the truth, I'm not feeling very special today."

So Sandy put Quest out into the exercise area, which had been vacated by Sarah and Puffin, and then set to work on the stable. For a while, Kay stayed. Then she said:

"I think I'll leave riding for today, Sandy. You can ride Quest if you like."

Sandy stopped work and looked at Kay. "You sure?" she asked, pushing back the fringe of her dark hair and extracting some straw. "That'll be great." Then, remembering that Kay was not well, she added, "Do you think you'll feel better tomorrow?"

"Well . . . I'm not sure. Tell you what, Sandy, if I'm not here by ten o'clock, you'd better take my place at Sue's official rehearsal."

"Poor Kay, she's not getting much riding, is she?" Mum commented that afternoon, during a lull between customers. "Last weekend she was away, and this weekend she's ill!"

Mum was talking through the bead curtains, behind which Sandy stood. Sandy's Saturday afternoon job was in this dim stockroom, where jars of sweets and boxes lined the walls. Her job was to weigh the sweets into bags, fasten them neatly with sticky tape, and label them with their correct prices, before stacking the packets on the central display cabinet in the shop. It was an uninteresting job in an uninteresting place, but Mum needed the help – and, besides, she paid Sandy five pounds pocket money for the afternoon's work. Sandy had a Building Society account which was growing, very slowly; an account which she hoped would buy a pony, one day – a pony just like Quest . . .

The little dark stockroom became less claustro-phobic as Quest entered through Sandy's imagination. The chestnut mare stood, pawing the ground and shaking her head, so that her long, fine fore-lock fell untidily about her delicately-moulded face, and those dark eyes flashed . . .

Sandy became aware of a question hanging in the air, and she came back from her imaginings to see Mum peering at her through the beads.

"You haven't been listening, have you, Sandy?" she said. "I've got such a day-dreamer for a daughter," she added, smiling nonetheless. For, when Mrs Corfield looked at her dark-haired younger daughter with the dreamy eyes, she remembered herself as a twelve-year-old, hanging over five-barred gates to catch just one quick glimpse of some pony in the distance, cropping the grass.

"What were you saying, Mum?"

Mrs Corfield, who had been about to grill her daughter in connection with her homework, mere-ly said, "Maybe I'll come and see this wonder pony tomorrow afternoon—"

"That'll be great," Sandy broke in. "Sue's having a dressage rehearsal – and if Kay's still not well, I'll be riding Quest!"

Passable was how Sue described the rehearsal. Everyone – even Sue herself – was a bit stiff and tense, and the ponies sensed the tension.

"You and Quest were the most relaxed," Sue told Sandy. "That was a *lovely* working trot – and your changes were smooth, too."

"That's just because I'm not actually going to be

doing it next week," Sandy replied, grinning. But, that evening, she lingered in the stable, while Quest munched at her feed. She told the chestnut how well-behaved she had been. "We're a team, now, aren't we, girlie?" she said – but her only reply was a contented grunt.

Maybe Sandy would have demanded a more decisive reply from the chestnut pony if she had known what Sue had in store.

As soon as Sandy arrived at the centre, after school on the following day, Chrissy pounced on her.

"Sue wants to see you in her office," she said, adding mysteriously, "straight away!"

"Why? What have I done?"

"Nothing – yet!"

"Chrissy! Stop being so dramatic. What's up?"

"Go and see Sue," Chrissy replied, annoyingly, "and then you'll find out!"

First, though, there was a detour to stable number eight, where Quest waited, her head hanging over the stable door, and her eyes watching eagerly for a sight of Sandy.

"Hello, gorgeous," said Sandy, offering an apple quarter, which was taken delicately from her hand and crunched appreciatively. Quest pushed against Sandy's arm and snorted her greeting. Promising to return soon, Sandy hurried on past the remaining stables, and through the door of the indoor school, towards Sue and Peter's office.

Andrea was in the riding area, banging her legs against Ragamuffin's sides as he trotted patiently round.

"Hello!" called Sandy, cheerily, and received a suspicious acknowledgment from the other girl.

Sue, having seen Sandy through the part-glass door, emerged from her office. "There you are, Sandy," she said.

"Chrissy said you wanted me."

Sue looked at her quizzically. "Can you jump?" she asked.

"On a pony, you mean," Sandy stammered foolishly, somewhat taken aback by the abruptness of Sue's question. "Yes, a bit. I did some at Crosslands, with Miss Middle. Nothing over about one foot six, though. Why?"

"Would you like to do some more jumping – do you like it?"

"Yes, but—"

"It's Kay, you see. She's just telephoned me. She wants you to take her place in the team!"

"But why?" Tessa asked the same question that Sandy had asked, just ten minutes earlier.

"She's heard from her doctor today – she's pregnant!"

Tessa paused to scrape the curry comb against the body brush, leaning against Duskie's shoulder as she said, "But people still ride, don't they – even when they're expecting babies?"

"I know, but apparently she had a miscarriage the last time, and the doctor doesn't think she ought to ride – at least for three months." Sandy twirled around with excitement. "I don't mind, anyway!" she said, happily. "Quest and I are going to be in the team!"

Her own words kept spinning in Sandy's mind at night, as she sat in bed, trying to learn her English homework. That evening, she and Tessa had practised the dressage movements during their ride. Now, with her English book in front of her, Sandy thought of Quest, hugging to herself the feeling of belonging which she felt with the chestnut pony.

"Oh, it's no good," Sandy said to herself, at last, pushing away the book in disgust. "I'll do it tomorrow."

As Sandy drifted slowly into a state of sleep, she remembered Andrea's face when she had heard Sue say, "Kay wants you to take her place in the team." She had been furious – that had been obvious. Even so, in some strange way, Sandy felt sorry for Andrea. She had tried to explain her feeling to Tessa, but Tessa had been adamant.

"You're crazy," she had said bluntly. "Andrea's just spoilt. You're wasting your time feeling sorry for her."

"But she misses out on everything. I mean, I try to be friendly, but she just won't be, will she?"

Tessa shrugged. "Well, why bother, then?"

"Oh, I don't know . . ." It seemed too difficult to explain to Tessa, who was part of a large family. Tessa had two younger sisters and an older brother. She probably could not understand how lonely it could be on your own – and how loneliness could turn to hostility. Sandy didn't even quite understand it herself. But, just sometimes, she felt sorry for Andrea.

There didn't seem too much time to do anything about Andrea. The days flew by, and the day of the dressage competition was getting uncomfortably close. Sandy began to wonder why she had worried about Andrea, anyway, since the other girl suddenly seemed a lot happier. She even seemed to be trying to improve her riding. On Friday evening, when Sue gathered the team together for a final practice, Sandy understood why.

"Well, that wasn't so bad," Sue said, when they had all taken the ponies through the test, "and Andrea – you go round, as well." She spoke to the others, as Andrea set off into the arena. "I've made Andrea reserve for the team," she explained.

Beside Sandy, Chrissy sighed. "I hope Sue's doing the right thing," she murmured. "She thinks it might improve Andrea's riding – but I'm not so sure."

"She *does* seem to be trying," said Sandy.

"*Very* trying!" commented Tessa tartly, from her other side.

"That *is* better." Adam spoke up from the other side of Chrissy. "That's quite a good canter."

"But Rags is a good pony!" Tessa pointed out.

"Well, anyway, she won't be riding unless one of us is ill," Sarah said. "And it might do her good," she added. "It has helped me, being part of the team."

As Andrea finished the test, her watchers gave her a round of applause. Her normally pale face turned pink with pleasure. "Was it all right?" she asked Sue.

"*Much* better," came the reply. "You're keeping

those legs under control – that's the main thing."

"She's turning to psychology," muttered Chrissy.

"Well, if it works –" Sandy countered.

Sue was calling to them all. "There you are, then, team! That's our last dressage practice before the big day. Chrissy and I will be here early on Sunday morning, but the rest of you – be ready, on the dot, at nine o'clock. We start promptly at nine thirty!"

7

"This is worse than exams at school," Sandy complained to Boxer, as she shivered in the cold light of dawn on Sunday morning. But, in reality, she knew that she was shivering with excitement.

Boxer ignored her completely. Curled up in a tight ball at the end of Sandy's bed, he obviously thought the hour much too early for any sensible person or cat to be up and about. Prowling and howling about the chimney pots of Clereton at two o'clock in the morning was a different matter. But five o'clock on a chilly grey May morning was not the best of times for Boxer, and his yellow eyes remained firmly shut behind his tabby tail, which curved neatly around his face.

Washing was normally a very hit and miss affair in the early mornings before leaving for the centre, but today Sandy took a little more care. She brushed her hair, too, and tried on the net which Sue had lent her, stifling her giggles in case she disturbed her mother in the next room. She packed clean jodhpurs, white shirt, tie and the hairnet carefully into a carrier bag, and dressed in jeans, an old sweater and trainers.

In the kitchen, her boots were waiting, shining from an energetic clean the night before. Sandy packed cotton and needles into her bag for sewing

Quest's plaits. She was determined that the chestnut pony was going to look as beautiful as possible. If nothing else, the Heronsway team was going to be clean and tidy – Sue had insisted on that.

Six o'clock already! Sandy whizzed round the tiny kitchen, pouring cereal and milk into a bowl, and then gulping it down in quick spoonfuls, at the same time preparing Mum's morning tea tray. While the kettle boiled, Sandy pulled her bike from the shed and stored the carrier bag safely in its capacious saddle bag, together with her boots, a packed lunch and a small bag of apple and carrot pieces for Quest. Then she made a quick dash back to the kitchen to make the tea.

"Have you got everything?" Mum asked sleepily, when Sandy arrived with the tray. Answered by a grunt, she added, "Good luck, then, love. I'll be over for the afternoon session – two o'clock, you said, didn't you?"

"Yes. Must go, Mum. See you."

Boxer had deigned to rouse himself and was stretching, lazily, in the kitchen, when Sandy returned.

"Sorry, Boxer. No time for your breakfast," she informed him as he began to lovingly circumnavigate her legs. "You'll have to suck up to Mum!" she added, extracting her legs from his weaving, purring body and letting herself out of the back door.

Tessa had just arrived at the end of the alleyway.

"Cold, isn't it?" she said.

"I think it's fright," Sandy observed.

"Mm. P'raps you're right."

The girls were unusually quiet during their cycle ride to the centre. A cold drizzle had begun to fall, and it was a relief to reach the warm stables. Soon, nerves forgotten, Sandy was humming to herself in Quest's stable, as she began grooming. Further down the row of stables, Tessa set to work on Duskie, and then Sarah arrived and disappeared into Puffin's stable.

An hour and a half of much brushing, plaiting and oiling later, three somewhat bedraggled girls emerged from the various stables, leaving behind three gleaming ponies, with plaited manes and tails. The girls congregated in the tack room, where Sue found them, sprawled untidily on the floor.

"What a scruffy-looking bunch," she said, grinning down at them. She had changed and was resplendent in her best riding clothes; her hair was tucked away neatly into a net.

Tessa looked at the others and winked. "Who is this woman?" she asked them, "Do we know her?"

"Come on," said Sue, laughing, "Let's have a coffee – and you can all change in the ladies."

To hide their nervousness, the girls giggled their way into their clean riding clothes and, amid much hilarity, tidied their hair away behind nets. Quarter of an hour later, they emerged and selfconsciously made their way to the coffee bar.

"Coffee on the house!" said Sue, cheerfully. "Now, I must get out and welcome our opponents!"

Through the window, the girls could see the horse boxes arriving, and their stomachs began to churn. Adam arrived, looking nervous, and even Chrissy, who poked her head round the door, seemed tense.

"I suppose we'd better get going." The normally exuberant Tessa sounded doubtful.

"S'pose you're right," said Adam, but no one moved. "Andrea's here, too," he observed, "and she's actually grooming her pony herself!"

This had to be seen to be believed! The junior section of the Heronsway team moved to the stables where Andrea was indeed busy forming Ragamuffin's mane into lumpy plaits.

"Rags looks lovely," said Sarah, who always managed to be kind.

Andrea looked up. "Plaiting's difficult, isn't it?" she said. "I can't seem to get them all the same – some are fatter than others."

"It looks OK," Tessa confirmed, "and hopefully you and Rags won't be needed, anyway."

"One of you might be ill," Andrea said, and it seemed to her listeners that she sounded almost hopeful!

"Come on," said Sue, arriving just then. "Time to saddle up and show your faces. Four other teams have arrived already, and there are four more to come!"

By the time the Heronsway competitors were mounted, there were ponies everywhere, as the teams unloaded and more teams arrived. The Heronsway team members eyed the opposition warily. From their nervous viewpoint, the others all looked like competitors at Badminton Horse Trials!

"Look at that team," Tessa hissed in Sandy's ear. "They're *all* wearing spurs!"

"Do you think it helps?"

"Dunno. But can you imagine Quest if *you* wore them?"

As she battled to control the chestnut mare, Sandy thought that Quest was bad enough *without* spurs. The close proximity of so many strange ponies was affecting her badly. She couldn't seem to keep still, and Sandy felt that at any moment her mount was going to take off like a rocket.

"Better take her away for a while," Sue advised. "I'll put you last in our team, so don't worry. Have a good ride on the lanes to calm her down."

So Sandy missed the beginning of the dressage competition. The early morning drizzle had given way to fitful sunshine. Quest danced down the lane for the first quarter of a mile, as Sandy had known she would. Then, gradually, she calmed down and Sandy let her walk freely on a loose rein. After half an hour, they turned for home. As they walked in at the entrance to the equestrian centre, a red mini turned in just ahead, coming from the opposite direction. Sandy recognized Kay in the driver's seat. At the end of the cinder path, the car stopped on the gravelled car park area, and Kay wound down the window.

"It's OK," said Sandy, before Kay had time to open her mouth, "I know I should be in there. I'm going to be doing my bit later on. I've just taken her out to calm her down."

"Of course. I should have guessed," said Kay. "See you inside, then. Good luck!"

Sandy found Tessa near the exercise area.

"How's it going?" she asked.

"Well, Chrissy's been in and Sue's going soon."

"How did Chrissy do?"

"Sue thinks it was OK. She was still a bit tense, but Merlin went well. How's Quest?"

"Better, I think."

"We'll just have to wait now," Tessa said. "You can't get into the indoor school. It's full of spectators and the horses waiting to go in soon."

Sue came over. She looked relaxed and smiling.

"You must have had your go," said Tessa.

"Yes. All over." She patted Beauty's neck. "She went well. Good old girl."

Beauty was Sue's own pony. She had bred her from her childhood pony, Trixie, a thirteen hand Dartmoor pony. "A real character," Sue had described her, "and as strong as an ox!" Beauty's father, apparently, had been a very handsome creature – a fifteen hand palomino Arab stallion. Sue had broken and trained Trixie's pretty dun filly, who had grown to be fourteen-two hands high, with the strength of her mother combined with the beauty and slightly dizzy disposition of her father. Now, at twelve, Beauty had sobered with maturity and, as well as being immaculately schooled, she was a powerful and fearless jumper.

"I hope I'm not going to let you down," said Tessa, dolefully.

"Me, too," said Sarah, who had arrived with Adam.

Sue looked round at them all. "Now listen to me," she said, firmly. "You won't let me down – *any* of you." She turned her head in the direction of a member of one of the other teams, a dark-haired girl mounted on a strong, bright bay pony. "Now, look at *that* girl," Sue said, with a cold glint in her eyes. "That's the kind that would let me down. That's a nice-looking pony she's riding, but she treats it like a *machine*! Just look at her!" The girls and Adam turned obediently to watch. The dark-haired girl was taking her pony round the practice area, obviously going through the dressage test. The pony was going well, but every time it appeared to do anything slightly wrong, the girl shouted at it, and jerked irritably at the reins.

"I'm sure that is a nice, easy-tempered pony," Sue continued, and there was anger in her voice. She turned back to her listeners. "Now, I chose you four because you're not like that. You care about the ponies – and that's the way it should be." She frowned slightly. "I'm not sure about Andrea," she admitted, "but I'm just hoping that she may change if we encourage her."

"Ponies have feelings," she continued. "They get frightened and they get cross, and they have days when they don't feel like doing much – just as we do. Now, our job is to encourage them – to tell them what we want and to ask them to do it." She smoothed Beauty's neck, looking down at her pony thoughtfully. "And if the pony doesn't do what we want, then it's *our* fault, not the pony's.

"So you see," she said, looking up again and smiling at them, "if something goes wrong today, you won't be letting me down. If you let anyone down at all, it will be your pony."

"Now, that's enough lecturing," Sue said. "Just go in there and enjoy it. You're all good enough to help your ponies to do really well. Adam, you're next in," she added, "because I need Jasper for a ride later on. Business has to go on, I'm afraid," she told him, ruefully. "I bet you're enjoying all this time with Jasper, aren't you?"

"It's brilliant!" Adam assured her enthusiastically.

"Enjoy yourselves," Sue repeated, as she moved away. "I must put Beauty in the stable and get back to the kitchen. All those visitors are going to be hungry at lunch time!"

The judges had devised a system by which the first member from one team should compete, followed by the first member of the second team, and so on, until one competitor from each of the nine teams had taken part. Then the second team member would compete, and the cycle would begin again. So, since Sandy was the last member of the Heronsway team, and Heronsway was the last team to take part, Sandy expected to take her turn at about three o'clock in the afternoon.

"I'm beginning to wonder why I got up so early," she said, yawning.

"I wish we could see what's going on," Tessa complained.

"It's getting less crowded," Sandy pointed out. "The competitors are taking their ponies away when they finish." She pointed towards the park for horseboxes, which had a wide surround of grass. "There are quite a few ponies tied up by the boxes, and I saw some going down the lane."

"Look. There's Adam. Let's see how he got on!"

Adam's thin face was glowing and he was grinning widely.

"You must have done well," Tessa pronounced, as they reached him.

"No, I didn't!" Adam declared. He patted Jasper, warmly. "But Jasper was great!"

"Well, what did you do wrong?"

Adam leaned back slightly in the saddle and pretended to hit himself on the head. "Just forgot to salute the judges!" he stated disgustedly. "That's all!"

"Will that lose many marks?" asked Sandy.

Adam shrugged. "I don't know," he admitted, "but I feel a fool. I mean, that's about the easiest thing to do in the whole test!"

Tessa giggled. "Jasper should have curtsied instead," she said.

Adam looked glum. "I hope I haven't spoiled our chances," he said, miserably. "We haven't been doing too badly. We're about fourth, so far, I think."

"How do you know?" Tessa demanded.

Adam looked at her. "Didn't you know?" he said. "The result sheets are pinned up in the school."

"We couldn't get in," Sandy explained.

"Well, I'm sure you can now," Adam said, as he moved away to take Jasper back to his stable. "Good luck!" he added.

Adam's good wishes were not needed just yet. When Sandy and Tessa managed to find a place in the indoor school, they saw that Sarah was about to begin her turn. Sarah was nervous, and her fear had communicated itself to Puffin, who worked his

70

way around the course stiffly and disjointedly at first. Then the two girls saw Sue move over to the fence and call out something to Sarah as she trotted past.

As the girls watched, they saw the tension fall away from Sarah. Sarah and Puffin circled at working trot and then, with a smooth change, they circled at working canter.

"She's off," Tessa whispered to Sandy, and now they could see that Sarah was concentrating on doing her best.

Puffin moved freely forward and cantered in a circle, changing at A, to canter round the arena. They finished the course smoothly and, it seemed to the two girls watching, faultlessly. Sarah trotted Puffin down the centre line, halted, saluted the judges, and left the arena beaming.

"That was great!" said Tessa, as Sarah and Puffin pushed their way through towards the two girls.

"He was *so* good!" said Sarah, patting Puffin enthusiastically.

"What did Sue say?" asked Sandy.

"She just told me to relax," Sarah explained, "and I remembered what she said to us."

"I'm next," said Tessa, her voice shaking.

"After eight others," Sandy pointed out, "*and* we'll probably have a break for lunch," she added.

"I can't bear the suspense," said Tessa, "I wish I could get it over with!"

But they had to wait. Four more competitors took part, and then Peter Venables' voice, over the loudspeaker system, announced a break of one and a half hours for lunch.

The girls put their ponies in the stables and joined the others in the tack room. There, sandwiches were consumed at a fast rate by the Heronsway competitors who had taken part, and nibbled nervously by the two still to compete.

"Tess, you can't still be trying to learn the course," Sandy said, as her friend pored over the sheet which gave details of the dressage test, nervously biting her nails as she did so.

"Supposing I forget!" Tessa looked up with anxious eyes.

"You won't," said Chrissy, who had just come in through the door. "Stop worrying so much. It's meant to be fun, you know!" She stood in the doorway and grinned down at them. "I've just looked at the sheets, and we're in third place now," she said. As shrieks of delight greeted her announcement, she added the warning, "but only just!"

8

"I haven't missed your turn, have I?" Mum asked.

Sandy shook her head.

"Sorry I'm late," Mum went on, chattily, "but it was your fault, really." Sandy raised her eyebrows questioningly, and Mum continued, "Dad came, you see, just as I was about to leave. He wanted to help with the kitchen cupboards. I didn't know *what* he was talking about – he said you told him I couldn't open them properly."

"I just told him they were sticky," Sandy said innocently, "and that you might like some help."

It was Mrs Corfield's turn to raise her eyebrows. "Sandy, I took those doors off *weeks* ago. The grooves just needed cleaning – they work beautifully now."

"Sorry. I didn't know. Dad didn't come with you, then?"

"No. He had some business meeting, he said. Sent his apologies. But Sandy—"

"Sorry, Mum. It's Tessa's turn. She's terribly nervous. I must go and wish her luck."

Sandy hurriedly moved away from her mother's questioning. She was disappointed that Dad hadn't come. She had hoped that maybe, if her parents had got together . . .

But now Tessa, her face determined, was making

for the entrance to the dressage area. As soon as Sandy saw Duskie trotting down the centre of the arena, she knew that he and Tessa would be all right. They completed their turn without any obvious mistakes, apart from some slight stiffness at changes of pace.

"That was really good," said Sandy, when Tessa and Duskie trotted over. "I wish I could have my go now."

"Look!" said Tessa, poking Sandy in the ribs, "It's that girl – the one that Sue pointed out."

The dark-haired girl was competing for Lollington Stacey Equestrian Centre. Riding the bay pony, she entered the arena at a trot and saluted the judges. Despite Sue's earlier comments, she and her pony completed the dressage amidst applause.

"She did really well," Sandy commented glumly.

"She didn't pat her pony," Tessa said.

"You don't get points for patting," Sandy declared, smoothing Quest's chestnut neck lovingly. "I bet that has put up their marks. Lollington Stacey are in first place at the moment."

At least Quest has calmed down, Sandy thought a little later, as she trotted Quest around just outside the dressage area. She leaned forward in the saddle and murmured into the chestnut pony's ear. "It's us now, girlie – and we've *got* to do well!"

The bell rang. Sandy's stomach jumped and seemed to turn over at least twice. It was her turn! Taking a deep breath, she turned her pony towards Marker A.

So far, so good, thought Sandy, as they trotted down the centre of the arena. Quest's working trot felt free and unhurried. She stopped beautifully and stood straight and still, with her head held well and her ears pricked, while Sandy saluted the judges. Quest flicked her ears back and responded well, trotting to C, where they tracked right and began the first circle from B.

Sandy forgot about her problem with Mum and Dad. She forgot that Kay was watching her pony perform; that Quest was inclined to buck. She forgot about everything except communicating to Quest through her legs and her whole self. In a dream-like state of concentration she persuaded the chestnut pony to walk, trot and canter smoothly and correctly through the test.

She awoke from her dream as they reached G, where Quest halted and Sandy saluted for the second and last time.

On a loose rein, Quest walked out of the arena, and Sandy became aware of a loud burst of applause.

Over the loudspeaker system came Peter's voice, announcing the end of the dressage competition. Sandy found herself surrounded by the other members of the Heronsway team.

"That was really great!" Tessa enthused.

"It wasn't any better than you and Duskie," Sandy protested.

"I've never seen Quest go so well." Sue, freed from her kitchen duties, appeared at Sandy's side, as she slid down from Quest's saddle.

"You *must* have improved our marks," Adam contributed.

Now, the indoor school was crowded again, as

competitors waited for the final scores to be pinned to the board. There was a break of half an hour, while the judges completed the last markings, and drank tea. Then, at last, the awaited marks were pinned to the board. A small cheer went up from the Lollington Stacey competitors.

"They must be first still," Tessa muttered to Sandy. Then, to Adam, who was nearer to the board, she called, "Can you see – what's our score?" Adam studied the board, and then pushed his way back to the others.

"We're still third," he said excitedly, "but our score is much better. We're only four points behind Turton Bridge Equestrian Centre, and eleven points behind Lollington Stacey!"

"So the first three are all quite close," said Sandy.

"Well done, team!" Sue called out, on her way to the judges' platform. "When they're all gone, we'll celebrate with chips and lemonade! See you all later on in the coffee bar – about 6 o'clock."

As Sandy tumbled into her bedroom that evening, at eight-thirty, she was hardly aware of anything except a huge desire for sleep. She pulled off her shirt and tugged at her jodhpurs, and then she saw her homework, looking at her accusingly from the bedside table.

"I can't – not tonight," Sandy yawned. Homework was such a nuisance. *School* was such a nuisance! There was no way that Sandy could force her eyes to stay open any longer. Homework would have to wait until tomorrow. Everything would have to wait until tomorrow . . .

"Sandra!"

Her foot on the first stair, Sandy froze. Whatever was up? Mum only ever called her by her full name when she was really annoyed. With a sigh, Sandy turned back towards the shop. Oh well, she supposed it would be just one more problem to add to a day of misfortunes.

It hadn't been a good day. This morning, while Sandy had been mixing Quest's breakfast in the feed room, the chestnut pony had somehow got loose and had wandered off towards the road. Sue had warned Sandy to be more careful, but Sandy had been *sure* that she had bolted the stable door securely.

Then, at school, she had been in trouble with Mr Foster, the English teacher, just because she hadn't done her homework. *Then* there had been Miss Townsend, her form teacher, nattering away to her about homework and getting into a good stream at the comprehensive school next term. She had had a day of being grumbled at, and now it looked as if it would be Mum's turn.

Sandy poked her head through the bead curtain. The shop was full of customers, so she stepped back into the stockroom, pressed the switch on the kettle and reached for the tea caddy. Maybe a cup of tea would soften Mum up . . .

"I've had a telephone call." Mum's eyes were accusing as she swivelled round on her stool to face her daughter.

"Who from?"

Mum looked across the top of her mug of

tea. The tea didn't seem to have done much good, Sandy thought regretfully.

"Miss Townsend," Mum replied, crisply. "She said—"

"I know, I know," Sandy broke in. She sighed. "I've had it all from her, too. I'm not working hard enough—"

"It's not your work at school, Sandy – although you're a bit dreamy," Mum interrupted. "It's your homework. You're just not *doing* it, Miss Townsend said. She said you're bright enough to be in the top stream when you move to the comprehensive, but you need to work harder this term. You don't have any past record with this school, you see, because you've only just started there this term. Unless you show them that you *can* work hard, the powers-that-be at the comp will put you in a low stream and see how you get on – that's what Miss Townsend said."

After she had telephoned to Tessa to explain that she would not be able to meet her at half past five as usual, Sandy pulled out her books from her school case.

She sat on her bed with her knees pulled up under her chin. She thought of Mum's ultimatum. Either the homework situation improved, or Sandy would have to stop looking after Quest until the holidays. But that might mean for ever, Sandy told herself dolefully. The competition would be over before the end of term, and then Kay's doctor might say that she could ride again – although she might still need help in the week, Sandy reminded herself. Mum had also insisted that Sandy could not leave for her evening session at the centre until she had completed at least half her homework – and then she must be home by eight o'clock to finish the rest.

Sandy scowled at her books. She wanted to feel angry and hard done by, but somehow she couldn't. She knew that Mum was right really. Sandy thought about her mother. She had seemed content lately. She enjoyed running the shop. In the evenings, she was busy with paperwork and ordering – and her newly-begun pastime of writing. She had sent off her article to a magazine and had started another.

Mum seemed happier now without Dad. But Sandy reminded herself quickly that she had decided to try to get them together again. It wasn't right that her parents had separated. *Other* people's parents didn't separate – well, most of them, anyway.

"How's it going?" Mum appeared in the doorway.

"It's this project." Sandy frowned. "I've got to write about businesses in our town and then choose one particular business to concentrate on. I thought I could write about the shop."

"Mm . . ." Mum sat down on the bed. "How much have you done, so far?" she asked.

Sandy reddened slightly. "Well . . . er . . . none yet."

Mrs Corfield tried hard to look stern, but in her heart she understood. "Tell you what," she said, after some thought, "how about doing the equestrian centre? Ask Sue and Peter all about their business."

Sandy suddenly came to life. She sat up straight on her bed. "Mum! You're fantastic! What a great idea! We have to write all about the business – and draw things. I can go and draw Quest, and still be doing my homework!"

As Mrs Corfield watched her younger daughter cycling away down the road after tea, she smiled to herself.

"Well, Boxer," she said, stooping to stroke the tabby cat, "I hope I've done the right thing."

Boxer gazed up at her foolishly, with adoring yellow eyes. It was his supper time!

9

"Think of our business as a donkey!"

In front of Sandy, Tessa twisted round in Duskie's saddle. "What *is* Sue talking about?" she hissed.

Sandy had other things to think about, as she struggled to keep Quest under control. "She's helping me with my homework," she panted.

Tessa looked mystified. "Well, you could've fooled me!" she declared.

"Off you go, Tessa!" Sue called. Tessa and Duskie set off towards the first jump in the indoor school, as Sarah and Puffin trotted out of the jumping area.

Sue joined Sandy at the edge of the school. Quest had quietened down, and was watching Duskie's progress with interest. As she, too, watched Tessa round the course of jumps, Sue continued her intriguing conversation. "You see, Peter and I wanted to build our equestrian centre," she said, "so we had to get the bank manager interested so that he would make us a loan. You would have to do the same with your donkey."

"But I haven't got—"

"*Your* bank manager," Sue continued, undeterred, "would lend you the money to buy your donkey, and then you could give rides on the sands which would earn you a living."

"Oh, I see . . . I think—"

"But," Sue continued, "out of that money, as well as paying back the money you borrowed for the donkey, you would have to pay the bank manager some money for letting you borrow his money – *and* you would need more money to buy food for your donkey and some for yourself, too." She stopped to call out "Steady, Tessa, not too sharp a turn or he'll – oh dear, he did!" Tessa had turned too close to the jump and Duskie had refused, skidding into the wall, knocking off several layers of bricks, and parting company with Tessa, who landed on the other side of the wall, still holding the reins.

"Sorry," said Tessa, standing up and brushing the sand off her knees, "that's not quite the idea, is it?"

"Not really," Sue admitted. "Try it again – and give him more room. He couldn't get a stride in before the jump was on him. You really can't blame him for refusing."

This time, Tessa and Duskie sailed over the wall together, and finished the small course without mishap.

"Now, Sandy," Sue said, "let's see how you get on with Quest."

The nearest Sandy had come to jumping Quest had been on one of their longer rides, when she and Tessa had found a low brush jump which some other rider had put across the path. Both ponies had hopped over the small obstacle easily. Sandy had remembered, then, how much she had loved the jumping she had done at Crosslands.

82

Now, she felt excited at the prospect of jumping this strong, lively pony which she adored so much. She wondered, as she turned the chestnut mare towards the first brush fence, whether Quest enjoyed jumping, too. She was left in no doubt. As Quest cantered towards the jump, Sandy could feel the strength and excitement thrilling through the pony. Shortening her stride, Quest leapt over the brush fence, snorting with pleasure as she landed. Picking up speed, she made for the spread, and flew over that.

Quest was getting more excited, and Sandy was finding it difficult to hold her. "Steady!" she warned, but Quest was enjoying herself too much to take any notice of Sandy's somewhat uncertain commands. Quest cut across the corner before the wall, and cleared this jump at an angle. From there, Quest took over, and Sandy sat in the saddle as they flew over each jump in turn. When they had cleared the last jump, Sandy managed, at last, to pull up her pony. Quest bucked on the spot, and danced sideways towards Sue.

"Well done, everyone," said Sue, since Sandy had been the last to jump. "That was a good start." She reached up and held Quest's reins while she spoke to Sandy. "You'll have to persuade Quest to take her jumping a little less wildly, Sandy. She's very enthusiastic – and a *very* good jumper, but she could spoil her chances if you're not careful." Turning back to the rest of the team, she said, "Lollington Stacey are very hot on jumping, I gather, but I'm sure we're just as good!"

Sandy walked Quest back to her stable. It was

half past seven already, and she had to spread the straw in the stable, give Quest a rub down and a feed, as well as re-fill her net with hay – *and* be home by eight o'clock.

While Tessa and Sarah trotted off down the cinder path for a short ride, Sandy completed her chores in record time. With a final hug for Quest, she hurried past the long row of stables, where some of the adult "do-it-yourselfers" were busy mucking out. Sandy made her way towards the hay barn, where her bicycle waited.

" 'Bye, Andrea," she called, but Andrea, who was half-heartedly brushing Ragamuffin's mane, kept her head averted, and seemed not to hear.

Well, at least she's looking after her pony more now, Sandy thought, as she pulled her bike from inside the barn. Recently, Andrea's mother had come to clean out the stable in the mornings only.

With her head down, battling against a strong wind, Sandy cycled down the lane towards the motorway bridge, planning her homework project. Back at the equestrian centre, Andrea closed Ragamuffin's stable door and bolted it carefully. She stroked her pony's nose, and then turned away, walking slowly towards the other row of stables.

"Sandy!"

Sue stood in the doorway, and called across the practice area from her office. "Can you come in here a minute?" she added.

In the office, Sue was surrounded by papers and books. Through the glass-topped door, which led into the indoor school, Sandy could see Peter and Chrissy putting up jumps.

"When can we have another practice?" Sandy asked.

Sue frowned slightly. "Well, *maybe* this evening. I'll have to see. I'm not sure if the school will be free. If not, I'll put up a couple of jumps in the exercise area for you – but I might not have time to be there myself. Chrissy will help you." She smiled. "We're *so* busy just now with lessons – which is good, of course."

"Plenty of donkey rides!" Sandy commented, grinning.

"So you *did* understand." Sue looked pleased. Then her smile faded. "Sandy, I'm afraid I've got to tell you off," she said.

"But what have I done?"

Sue frowned again. "Well, I can't see what else it can be. I think you must be getting careless, Sandy."

"But, what—"

"Quest was loose again, yesterday evening."

"What!" Sandy exclaimed.

"And you *were* in a hurry, weren't you?" Sue reminded her.

"Yes, but not *that* much of a hurry," Sandy protested. "I bolt her in *really* carefully, every time."

"Well, Sandy, you can't have – not last night, anyway." Sue continued, her voice serious, "I can't risk any accidents. You *must* be more careful. If anything were to happen to Quest. I would be responsible to Kay."

"But, Sue—"

85

"I *must* get on now," Sue interrupted. "Just be more careful." The urgent ring of the telephone claimed Sue's attention, and Sandy walked away dejectedly towards the stables.

"Are you sure?"

Tessa and Sandy had met at the manure heap, each with a wheelbarrow of soiled straw and Sandy had told her friend about her conversation with Sue.

"Of course I am!"

"You *were* in a terrific hurry . . ."

"Tess, I *know* I bolted that door. And it's the *second* time."

"P'raps she's learned to push back the bolt," Tessa suggested, doubtfully. "They do, sometimes."

"Hmp. A bit unlikely, I think," Sandy commented. "She would have to put her head over the door and work at it with her chin," Sandy continued, drily. "Then she'd have to pull the bolt handle up before she pushed it along. I don't think it's possible," she concluded.

"What do you think happened, then?" Tessa demanded.

"Someone is letting Quest out of her stable," said Sandy, dramatically, tipping her contribution onto the heap as she spoke, and then propping her wheelbarrow next to Tessa's.

Tessa gaped at her. "But why on earth would someone want to do that?"

"That's what I can't puzzle out," Sandy admitted. The two girls walked slowly back to the stable block.

"All I can think," Sandy continued, "is that someone is trying to steal her – and then gets cold feet about it!"

"P'raps Kay could throw some light on it."

"No! I don't want to tell Kay," said Sandy, hastily. "She might decide to stop letting me look after Quest."

"Well then," said Tessa, stopping and facing her friend, with a determined expression on her face, "we'll have to keep guard!"

"But *I* can't!" wailed Sandy. "I'm confined to barracks from eight o'clock every evening to do my homework!"

Tessa stared at the ground, as if the concrete might hold the answer. "We'll have to enlist the others to help," she said at last, looking up.

"But no one is going to want to stay here too late."

"I give up!" Tessa said, exasperated. "Padlocks, then!"

Sandy shook her head. "Sue won't allow padlocks – in case of fire," she said.

"Well, let's call a meeting of the Heronsway team, anyway," Tessa suggested, "and get everyone to keep a good look-out. After all, whoever it is might try to steal one of *our* ponies, instead!"

So, that evening, Sandy and Tessa met in the coffee bar, gathering in Sarah, Adam, Chrissy and Andrea on the way. They explained the situation, and everyone promised to help.

"But you're sure," Chrissy asked Sandy, "it wasn't just that you forgot—"

"No! It wasn't!" Sandy interrupted, exasperated.

"OK. OK," Chrissy said, hastily. "We'll help,
won't we, team?"

10

That was the trouble with Dad, Sandy decided, as she gave her hair a perfunctory brush and reached for her anorak. Most of the time, when you wanted him, he was off here, there and everywhere. Then, when you were busy, he arrived, smiling and cheerful, to whisk you off somewhere.

"Ready?" Dad's face appeared round Sandy's bedroom door. "I like your room," he added. "It's cosy. Plenty of posters – you can't mistake what it is that you like, Sandy."

Sandy pointed to the large poster on the wall opposite her bed. She gazed at it every night before she went to sleep.

"That one's just like Quest," she said.

"Ah. I seem to have heard that name before. Come on, then, or we'll be late."

He was always in a hurry, Sandy thought, as she followed Dad down the narrow stairs and through the shop. With a quick wave to Mum, they were out through the door and into Dad's car.

Sandy felt guilty as she leaned back in the passenger seat. It was Saturday afternoon – the time when she worked in the stock room, packing sweets to earn her pocket money. Dad had arrived, out of the blue, to take her with him for the afternoon, and Mum had said that she could manage.

"But Mum, I haven't finished," Sandy had protested.

"I can cope here. You go on. You don't see Dad very often, these days, do you?"

Sandy had thought that perhaps she could continue with her plan to bring her parents together again, so she agreed. But Dad was always in such a hurry and had so much to talk about, that Sandy couldn't get the conversation round to him and Mum.

"Last time I visited these customers," Dad was saying, raising his voice slightly above the roar of the car as it sped down the motorway, "I saw this riding centre, and I thought I would bring you and treat you to a ride the next time I came."

It turned out to be Ludleigh Equestrian Centre, one of the centres taking part in the competition. On the previous Sunday, their team had finished in fourth place behind Heronsway.

But Dad hadn't thought about booking, of course.

"Sorry," said the woman behind the desk in the office. "We're completely booked up today." She looked hard at Sandy. "Haven't I seen you before?" she asked. "Weren't you riding that bouncy chestnut last Sunday?" When Sandy nodded, the woman added, "Very nice animal, that – the sort I like. Got a bit of spirit, but kind, too."

"Well, Sandy," said Dad, impatient to get away to his customers, "I'm sorry – I should have thought to book. What will you do with yourself while I'm at work?"

"You can stay here if you like," said the woman.

She smiled at Sandy. "Size up the opposition! We're out to get you next time, you know. We're only eight points behind you – *and* we'll be on home ground!"

Sandy spent two hours wandering round Ludleigh Equestrian Centre, happy enough to be within sight and sound of horses, but wishing that, instead, she could be at Heronsway with Quest.

"So it wasn't a particularly successful afternoon?"

Chrissy was leaning over the stable door, that evening, while Sandy brushed the last of the dirty straw on to the spade, and emptied it into the barrow. Sandy straightened up.

"Well, I suppose it was OK, seeing Ludleigh," she admitted, "It's even bigger than here!" Sandy smoothed Quest's soft nose thoughtfully. The lively chestnut was quiet; she was tied up outside her stable, her head resting on the lower door, idly watching while Sandy prepared her bed for later on.

"Chrissy . . ." Sandy obviously had something on her mind.

"Yes?"

"You don't think – I mean, I know it sounds stupid, but you don't think that woman from Ludleigh is trying to *steal* Quest? She said how much she liked her—"

Chrissy's peal of laughter echoed in the stable depths, and Quest turned her head sharply, looking at the older girl with inquisitive eyes.

"You're getting much too imaginative," Chrissy laughed. "Perhaps we ought to make a bed up for you in Quest's stable," she chuckled. Then, seeing Sandy's worried face, she added, kindly, "If you take my advice, Sandy, forget it! I don't suppose it'll happen again. I really don't think Mrs Marran from Ludleigh is going to travel fifty miles to steal Quest, and then go away without her!

"Let's have some jumping practice," she said, moving away towards Merlin's stable. "I can't stay long this evening – it's my late night at the pub. Sarah and Andrea are in there already, and Tessa and Adam are nearly ready."

Sandy had been practising throughout the week, and had gradually encouraged Quest to approach the jumps more thoughtfully. Still, the chestnut mare liked to jump at speed.

"Don't try to stop *that*," Sue had advised, "It's the way she goes best – and that's good in competitions. What you need to persuade her to do is get her strides the right length between jumps, so that she leaves the ground at the right distance from the jump. She can't just rush round, throwing herself wildly at the jumps! She obviously *loves* jumping, so she must learn to do it properly!"

Sue had set up a full course in the indoor school. When Sandy arrived, Andrea and Ragamuffin were halfway round the course. Sandy was surprised to notice that Andrea was riding quite well.

"Good!" Sue, who had just entered the school riding Beauty, stopped to applaud. "You're improving, Andrea. That was a really good round – and fast, too."

Andrea, usually so sullen, was smiling broadly.

She patted her pony enthusiastically. "*Good* boy, Rags," she said.

Tessa looked across at Sandy. Perhaps Andrea's not so bad, after all, her expression said.

Andrea trotted Ragamuffin over to Sue. "Well, then . . ." she wheedled, "couldn't *I* be in the team, now?" She pouted, "It's not *fair*," she complained.

"Andrea." Sue spoke sharply. "I've chosen the team, and it stands as it is for the competition. I'm sure there will be *other* competitions, and I'll consider you then. You are our reserve for this competition, which is quite an important position. If anything happens to one of the ponies or riders, then I shall ask you and Ragamuffin to take their place. Now, I don't want to have to keep explaining."

Andrea moved Ragamuffin to one corner of the school, where she sat sulking while the others practised. Tessa looked across at Sandy again, and raised her eyes heavenwards. Poor Andrea, Sandy thought, she can't help having been spoilt – but she *was* a pain at times!

After the jumping practice, which Sue pronounced a successful one, Sandy settled Quest in for the night. She gave her a feed, filled her net, and made sure that her automatic drinking bowl was working. She put her arms round the mare's neck, resting her head against Quest's long, thick mane.

"Now, if anyone comes to let you out, except me," she murmured into Quest's ear, "just don't go. Stay here and wait for me." But Quest was not paying attention. Having finished her feed, and pushed her bucket round and round the stable in order to extract the last possible crumb of food, she was now munching steadily and meditatively at her hay.

As Sandy let herself out of the stable, carefully checking the bolting of the door, Adam appeared.

"I can stay on a bit this evening," he told Sandy, "so I'll keep an eye on Quest's stable, if you like."

"Thanks," said Sandy, gratefully. "I'm sure the others think I'm being stupid worrying about her," she added. "They think I'm careless."

"But you're not, though," Adam said, quickly. "I saw you, just now, bolting the door."

"Well, if you *are* staying—"

"There'll be nobody at home, you see," said Adam. "Nick's gone to a motorbike rally for the weekend, and Dad's at a farm. He's expecting a cow there to have a difficult birth, and he might be home late."

"Your dad's a vet, isn't he?"

Adam nodded. "He works all hours," he said.

"What about your mum?"

Adam's brown eyes darkened with pain, and he pushed back his hair in an effort to hide his feelings. He said abruptly, "She died last year."

"Oh – I'm sorry."

There was a small silence. Then Adam said, "Don't worry about Quest. I'll be here for an hour or two yet." His face brightened. "I'm going to clean Jasper's tack for Sue," he added.

"You're doing quite a lot of work around the stables," Sandy remarked.

"Well, I'm having so much extra riding with

this competition, I feel I want to help to pay for it."

"That's great, then, if you're staying on," said Sandy. "My curfew hour draws near!" she added, ruefully. "I'll have to get home to do my project." She told Adam about her troubles at school, and Mum's ultimatum.

"You're lucky," said Adam glumly.

"Lucky?"

"I want to go to the comprehensive next term."

"And can't you?"

Adam gave a deep sigh. "Dad wants me to try for the grammar school," he said despondently. "And that'll mean travelling twelve miles every morning and evening – *and* school on Saturday mornings! I shall hardly have any time for riding!"

"That does sound awful," Sandy agreed. "Can't he be persuaded against it?"

"I'm doing my best," Adam admitted. "I've told him how cut off I'll be. All my friends are here, in Clereton. Trouble is, *he* went there, you see."

"Maybe you'll change his mind," said Sandy, encouragingly. "I'd better go now," she added. "Thanks for watching Quest for me."

Cycling home, through the lanes, where the spring grass was bursting with wild flowers, Sandy thought about Adam's school problem. She realized how lucky she was to be so close to school, and to be able to cycle out, easily and quickly, to the equestrian centre. Some owners, like Kay, had to travel quite a distance to see and ride their horses.

When she got home, Sandy shut herself away in her bedroom and worked hard on her project. She had to admit that she was enjoying it. She had cycled round Clereton during the week, noting down all the various businesses, writing about them for her project and drawing a plan of the town and where most businesses were situated. Now, she had begun on the equestrian centre.

"That's coming on well," said Mum, when she came up with coffee and biscuits. She had brought her own mug of coffee, too, so she sat down on the end of Sandy's bed to inspect the work.

Sandy told Mum about Adam's school difficulty.

"Poor boy. It *is* quite a problem."

"You wouldn't do that to me, would you?" Sandy asked anxiously. Mum shook her head. "I tend to agree with Adam," she said. "He won't have proper friends if he goes that far to school – he'll only see them in school time. Besides," she added, "I had another call from Miss Townsend this evening. She says you have worked really hard this week. She's hoping you'll keep it up."

"I will, don't worry!"

As the light faded in Sandy's attic room, she worked on until tiredness overcame her. Tomorrow was Sunday, her favourite day. Her homework done, she could spend all day with Quest.

11

Weekends were usually particularly busy at the equestrian centre. Most of the twenty-five full livery horses were ridden by their owners who were at work during the week. The "do-it-yourself" owners took longer than usual over their morning mucking-out sessions, being able to lean on their brushes and chat instead of having to rush away to work or school.

Kay Carter visited Heronsway on the following Saturday. She watched the final jumping practice in the morning, which was fitted in between lessons.

"Everyone seemed to do very well," Kay said to Sandy, after the jumping practice. "Quest's doing well, just now. She seems . . . steadier, but she still managed to nip round that course at a pretty good pace!"

Kay had treated Sandy to a coffee and a snack, and Sandy nodded her agreement from behind a massive bacon sandwich as she watched Sue giving a lesson in the indoor school. Sue's pupil – a woman of fifty or so – was attempting a small course of jumps on a beautiful dark bay gelding of about sixteen hands. While Sue gave jumping and dressage lessons on Saturday mornings to some of the livery owners in the indoor school, Peter took out a group of ten riders on some of the centre's own horses for a longer three-hour ride.

Sandy leaned back in her chair, enjoying the comfort of the coffee bar. This, too, was a busy place at the weekends, with Chrissy or Sue doling out mugs of coffee, bacon sandwiches and chips. As she looked round her, Sandy thought, ruefully, that the equestrian centre's coffee bar was probably three times the size of the tiny living room at the shop – and three times more luxurious, too! At one end was the bar from which Chrissy was dispensing food and drinks. At the other end – closed at present – was the wine bar, which Peter opened in the evenings for the adult clients. On the opposite wall from where Sandy and Kay sat, a red-brick fireplace shone with an array of horse brasses which hung across the top and down each side.

Swallowing her last mouthful of sandwich, Sandy turned to Kay, remembering again the draughty old stables at Crosslands. "Yes," she said to a slightly surprised Kay, "and she's a lucky pony, to be living here at Heronsway."

Sandy worked in the shop on Saturday afternoon, and after tea she and Tessa went for a ride along the tracks.

"We'll forget about jumping for a bit," suggested Tessa.

"Good idea," Sandy agreed. "All my dreams, at the moment, are jumping ones. The jumps get bigger and bigger. Either that, or Quest shrinks!"

The girls decided not to be late back that evening, since they would be making a very early start the next day. So by seven-thirty the ponies had been fed, and were knee-deep in clean straw.

The tack had been cleaned the night before, but Sandy and Tessa spent twenty minutes cleaning the bits and stirrup irons, and rubbing up the leather.

"Thank goodness we don't have to plait the ponies' manes and tails tomorrow," said Tessa. "We'd have to be here in the middle of the night!"

Then, with a lingering farewell to the ponies, the two girls left together, cycling through the lanes and parting at the High Street. Boots had to be cleaned and coats brushed for the following day.

Sandy had decided to have an early night, so she made her way to her bedroom before nine o'clock, and she was asleep before the light had faded from the sky.

Sandy awoke with a start. It was dark. She wondered what had woken her. She felt the end of her bed, but there was no warm, furry ball – otherwise known as Boxer – sleeping there. Sometimes, Boxer would jump onto the roof outside Sandy's window, from the high wall opposite. If the window was open, he would squeeze his fat, tabby self through the opening and make his way to the end of Sandy's bed. There, purring to himself, he would form a comfortable nest in the duvet, pounding his fat paws until all felt well, and then curl up for sleep. If the window was not open, however, Sandy would be called from her sleep by a plaintive yowl – or several plaintive yowls if she were inconsiderate enough to be deeply asleep!

Sandy listened. No yowls. She got out of bed and padded over to the window. Pulling back the curtain, she peered out. No, it couldn't have been Boxer. The red-tiled roof was bathed in moonlight, but no tabby cat waited there.

Sandy went back to bed and cuddled down again into the warmth. But she couldn't sleep. Somehow, she felt uneasy. She lay awake, her eyes slowly growing accustomed to the darkness. They picked out the poster on the wall – her favourite one of the rearing chestnut horse. She turned away, clamping her eyes firmly shut.

At last, she sat up in bed. It was no good. She couldn't sleep. She was sure that something was wrong – somehow she felt that she should go to see Quest. Of course, it was a ridiculous idea. Mum would say "Don't be crazy – go back to bed and get some sleep." But she *couldn't* sleep – and now she felt that she *must* see Quest!

For the second time that night, Sandy gave up her warm bed for the slightly chilly air of a May night. She had made up her mind – she *would* go and see Quest. She pulled on jeans and a sweater on top of her pyjamas. She picked up her trainers and lifted her jacket from the hook behind the bedroom door.

Sandy opened her door quietly. The house was in darkness. Carefully, she crept down the stairs, avoiding the third from the top which always creaked. Downstairs, in the kitchen, she helped herself to a banana, having found that sleuth work in the middle of the night made her hungry! She looked at the kitchen clock. It was eleven-thirty. Slipping into her trainers and

100

jacket, she thrust a carrot into her pocket for Quest.

As she lifted her bicycle carefully from its resting place in the shed, Sandy wondered, for a moment, whatever she was doing, rooting about in the shed at nearly midnight on a moonlit night. Mum would have forty fits if she could see her!

Sandy had never realized before that her front wheel squeaked! Holding the offending wheel off the ground, she pushed her bike out of the back yard and down the dark little alleyway. She was glad to reach the end, and find that the street lights were still on. Even the dustbins in the alleyway had looked menacing!

The centre of Clereton – known affectionately by people who lived there as "the village" – was practically deserted. Even on Saturday nights, nothing much happened in this small town. But for the equestrian centre, Sandy thought, as she circled the clock tower and turned towards the moors, she and Tessa might grumble at the quietness of their town.

A couple of late-night revellers from the "Waggoner's Rest" drifted down the road, but apart from these the roads were deserted as Sandy's bike bounced along in solitary state. At the roundabout, she turned her bicycle off the main road into the lane. Here, the darkness of the night seemed to intensify. The moon had disappeared suddenly behind a cloud, leaving the beam from Sandy's bicycle lamp as her sole source of light. She pedalled slowly, watching the edge of the lane carefully. Then the welcome lights of the motorway traffic appeared in front of her, and Sandy knew that she had reached the motorway bridge. She cycled over the bridge, looking down to see the lights rushing past below her.

As she freewheeled down from the bridge, Sandy thought for a moment that she heard the sound of horses' hooves, clip-clopping on the metal road. But she was being fanciful, she told herself, pedalling harder. Nobody was out riding at midnight.

Then Sandy's throat went dry with fright, as she remembered a gory tale that Tessa had told her of a phantom horseman, who haunted the moorland lanes at midnight on moonless nights! The rider – a highwayman, of course – had been ambushed and killed by several of his victims who had ganged together about two hundred years ago, at just this spot on the moors. Tessa had taken great relish in recounting the legend to her credulous friend one lunch time break when the weather had been too wet for them to go outside. Then, Sandy had felt a prickly sensation in her scalp. Now, she was petrified! She stopped her bicycle and stood, uncertain which way to run! She turned her bicycle wheel to the right, so that the light shone across the road. The beam picked out a vague shape, and Sandy's heart stood still. Then the shape moved slightly and Sandy's heart pounded against her ribs.

Suddenly, relief flooded over her. Sandy knew that shape only too well. Two large brown eyes looked at her in surprise below a long, wispy forelock and two neat, pricked ears. Quest's white blaze shone out in the darkness.

102

Sandy threw down her bicycle and flung her arms around the surprised pony's neck.

"Questie! You naughty girl," Sandy murmured, fondly. "Whatever are you doing here?"

Sandy stood back, noticing that Quest was wearing a headcollar, with the lead rope hanging down loosely. "What on earth —" Sandy began. Then, as suddenly as it had gone, the moon reappeared from behind the cloud, sailing across clear sky and illuminating the empty moors.

But the moors were not empty. Sheep, lying together in the field next to the lane, turned their heads to study Sandy and Quest with wise but startled eyes. And there was something else. A slight movement in the hedge caught Sandy's eye. Her heart began to pound again, as another shape became apparent – a human shape, huddled against the hedge.

Made brave by the nearness of the chestnut pony, onto whose back she could leap and escape from this new phantom, Sandy took a step forward.

"Who is it?" she demanded. "Who's—" With a sharp intake of breath, she recognized the figure. "Andrea!" she gasped.

12

Andrea scrambled out from the hedge, and the two girls stared at each other in the moonlight. It was Andrea who broke the silence "I – I was just taking her back to her stable," she stammered.

"But – what was she doing here?"

"She must have . . . escaped . . ." Andrea's voice trailed away, as Sandy took a step forward. Sandy stared hard at the other girl.

"Of course," she said, at last. "It was *you*, wasn't it?" Her voice was cold. "I've been so stupid," she continued, bitterly, "thinking it was Mrs Marran from Ludleigh. I even began to wonder if I *was* being careless, like everyone thought."

"I was taking her back," Andrea repeated, miserably, "*really* I was."

Sandy took hold of the other girl by the shoulders. "How *could* you?" she demanded, shaking Andrea angrily. "Quest might have got on to the motorway. She might have been—" Sandy's voice choked, as her vivid imagination visualized Quest's lifeless and mutilated body thrown by a passing car onto the grass verge at the side of the motorway. "How could you, how *could* you?" she repeated furiously.

"I was taking her back," was all Andrea could sob, and now Sandy's anger disappeared. She stopped shaking the other girl, and spoke quietly. "But why let her out in the first place?" she asked, exasperated.

"I wanted her to be lost," Andrea sniffed, avoiding Sandy's eyes, as she looked down at the ground, "just until after tomorrow."

"But—"

"I wanted to be one of the team – in the jumping."

"And you put Quest's life at risk – and perhaps people's lives, too, if there had been an accident – just for that?"

Andrea looked up, her face red and swollen from crying. "But I suddenly realized, when I got home, what I'd done," she explained, "and I came back. She would have been all right, and you wouldn't have known if you hadn't come," she added miserably.

Their conversation was disturbed by an impatient chestnut face pushing between them. Quest snorted and moved her head restlessly against Sandy's arm.

Sandy suddenly realized how tired she was. "We'd better get Quest back to her stable," she said flatly.

The two walked on along the lane in silence, Sandy leading the chestnut pony and Andrea pushing the bicycle. When they reached the cinder path, Sandy said, "I'll try and keep to the grass as much as possible – we don't want to wake Sue and Peter."

"I suppose you'll tell Sue," Andrea said sorrowfully. "She won't want me to stay on at the centre, will she?"

There was silence, with only the sound of Quest's hooves thudding softly against the cinder path. Sandy thought hard. She still felt sorry for this spoilt, lonely girl. After all, Quest *had* been facing in the direction of Heronsway, so Andrea had been telling the truth when she said that she was taking the chestnut mare home.

"I don't think so," Sandy said, at last. She stopped and turned towards the other girl. "But you won't ever do it again, will you?" she said. Andrea shook her head.

"I don't understand you, Andrea," Sandy said, as they started off again towards the stables. "You've got your own pony – and he's lovely. You're so lucky."

"I wanted to do the jumping." Andrea's voice was wretched.

"But Sue told you that next time perhaps you'll be in the team."

"I know."

"Well, then . . ."

By skirting round the grassy edge of the yard, they managed to reach Quest's stable with only a few steps on the concrete, which were negotiated slowly without too much clatter.

Sandy put Quest into her stable. She had removed her bicycle lamp and brought it with her. She shone the beam of the lamp on to the pony, running it up and down the chestnut's legs and over her body and head.

"She seems to be all right, anyway," she conceded. "No scratches or anything."

"I'm sorry," Andrea said.

"But why—"

Both girls were whispering in the dark stable.

"I wanted to do something to make you all like me," Andrea replied. "I thought if I took part in the jumping competition—"

"But everyone *will* like you if you just join in a bit more," Sandy interrupted.

"My riding's hopeless, though. You all think I'm stupid."

"No, we don't. A bit spoilt, maybe." Sandy felt weary, but she tried to explain. "You've got to learn to do things for yourself, Andrea," she said, "and not expect to have everything you want just like that. Sue said you were riding much better at the jumping practice. Maybe, soon, she'll think you're good enough to take part in competitions. Oh, come on," Sandy added, her voice heavy with tiredness, "let's get home. I've set my alarm for five o'clock."

Despite her tiredness, Sandy did not find it easy to sleep when, at last, she tumbled back into her bed at one-thirty that morning. Again and again Quest would enter her mind, trotting across the grass verge at the side of the motorway, wandering on to the hard shoulder and then on to the motorway itself. She would turn her beautiful head, her brown eyes at first puzzled and then blinded by the oncoming lights. Frightened and confused, she would turn, first one way and then the other, calling with a terrified whinny before plunging into the path of the oncoming car . . .

Her heart pounding, Sandy would sit up quickly

in bed, realizing that she had dropped off to sleep and, again, had been having a nightmare. At last she was so exhausted that the chestnut pony no longer invaded her thoughts, and she slept deeply for the last few hours before her alarm woke her shrilly at five o'clock.

"You look worn out, Sandy," Mum said at six o'clock, when Sandy arrived with the usual tray of tea. "Couldn't you sleep, either?" Mum propped herself up on her elbows and blinked at her daughter sleepily. "I kept hearing noises last night," she said, "but I was too tired to investigate. Did you hear anything?"

Sandy shook her head, smiling inwardly at the thought of Mum's face if she knew where her younger daughter had been at one o'clock in the morning!

"I'll tell her one day," Sandy promised herself, "but not now."

The journey to the equestrian centre, through pouring rain, woke Sandy up a little, and she arrived at the hay barn dripping wet but cheerful. She pushed her bicycle into the barn, next to Tessa's, and made her way quickly to Quest's stable. With a huge sense of relief, she saw the well-loved chestnut head watching for her from stable number eight. Quest whinnied, tossing her head up and down.

Thank goodness Quest did not seem tired after her adventure, Sandy thought, as she let herself into the stable and put her arms round the pony's neck. But there was no time for petting. The stable needed mucking out and Quest had to be fed, groomed and prepared for the horsebox.

Sue came round to each stable. "I want them over by the horseboxes by seven-fifteen," she warned them. "Then if there's any trouble with boxing any of them, we'll have some time in hand." But all the ponies were used to being boxed, and there were no hitches. Even Quest marched up the ramp without batting an eyelid. The seven ponies were safely in the two horseboxes and everyone was ready to leave well before eight o'clock.

"Fine," said Peter. "We can take it easy on the motorway. No rushing!"

Andrea had kept out of Sandy's way. Sandy had seen her arrive, and had been surprised to see that Andrea's mother had not been there to clean out the stable. Andrea had disappeared into Ragamuffin's stable and had re-emerged at seven o'clock, with Rags rugged and prepared for the box. She had ventured an anxious glance in Sandy's direction, and Sandy had managed an encouraging smile. She did not feel very inclined to talk to Andrea this morning, but soon found herself bundled into the front of the horse box by Peter, packed tightly between Tessa and Andrea.

Tessa, who was in a cheerful, exuberant mood, was surprised when her two companions nodded off as soon as David got the vehicle under way.

"You two aren't much company," she grumbled. She dug Sandy in the ribs. "Wake up! You've got to be wide awake and fit for tackling that jumping course at Ludleigh."

Sandy groaned. "Don't remind me," she said, her eyes closing, "I must get some sleep first."

Tessa turned her chatter upon Peter, as the other two slept. "Don't know what's the matter with those two," she complained, "Anyone would think they'd been up half the night!"

The first sight of Ludleigh was impressive. Two large, painted signs flanked a wide, tarmacked entrance through which the horseboxes entered.

Tessa woke Sandy to show her.

"I know, I've seen it before," Sandy murmured, sleepily.

At the horsebox park, Mrs Marran was there to greet them. Sandy forced herself to wake up properly to smile a greeting. After all, she felt that she should apologize to Mrs Marran!

"Come on," Sue called, when the boxes had been parked. "Let's get the ponies out and give them a chance to stretch their legs. They don't want to be stiff for the jumping!"

As more boxes arrived, the Heronsway team members led their ponies down the ramps and walked them round the field next to the park. The ponies were suspiciously excited in their new environment.

Chrissy began to saddle up. "I'm first in for Heronsway," she said, checking the girth before mounting her pony. "I'm going to have a go at that practice jump."

"We can walk the course now," Sue reminded her.

"OK. I'll be there in a jiffy," Chrissy replied. "I'll hand Merlin over to Peter in a moment and follow you in."

The indoor school was slightly larger than the one at Heronsway. And somehow, Sandy thought, as she walked the course with Tessa, the jumps seemed bigger, too.

"It's because we're down on the ground, not on the ponies," Sue assured her. "The biggest is the wall, and that's only two foot nine."

"Only! That's the highest I've jumped," Sarah said, anxiously. "I'm sure it's bigger than that. It looks huge!"

"Better saddle up," Sue advised. "Have you all got the course sorted out?"

Tessa, always afraid of forgetting the course, walked round it again, while the others went to saddle up their ponies.

"Don't practise too much!" Sue called out, as they left.

The indoor school at Ludleigh had wide windows all down one side, which enabled most of the waiting competitors to be able to watch the competition. From their position by one of the windows, the junior section of the Heronsway team watched as Chrissy took Merlin round the course. They completed the nine obstacles without any jumping faults.

"That's a great start," said Adam. "It looked fast, too."

"Lollington Stacey seemed about the same," said Tessa, biting her nails nervously. The first competitor for Ludleigh had also jumped a fast clear round.

Tessa spoke again, and her normally cheerful

face was serious and determined. "I'm *going* to do a good round," she said, grimly.

The others looked at each other.

"Me, too," said Adam. "We've got to do well – for Sue. She's spent such a lot of time with us."

A spirit of silent determination surrounded the Heronsway team, as Sue trotted up to a quiet, subdued group.

"What's the matter, team?" she asked, cheerily, "Aren't you pleased? Chrissy's was the best of the clear round times in that first set!"

Sandy was surprised at how quickly the competition was progressing. As Adam left for the indoor school, his face resolute, Sandy found Sue and questioned her. Sue, who had jumped a fast clear round on Beauty, had unsaddled her pony and was tying her up by the horseboxes.

"Isn't the competition going to finish rather early?" Sandy asked her.

Sue looked at her in surprise. "You obviously didn't hear the announcement at the beginning," she replied. "We're going to do this course, and then they're going to raise the jumps and we'll all do it again!"

13

As the time for her turn approached, Sandy became more and more nervous. All the members
of the Heronsway team had done well, and Sue,
who was working out the marks as each competitor
took a turn, thought that Heronsway and Turton
Bridge were about level, behind Lollington Stacey,
with Ludleigh breathing down their necks in fourth
position.

"Don't forget we have to do it all again, but
higher!" she warned.

Sandy sat hunched miserably on Quest. A wave
of tiredness swept over her. She had never felt
less like jumping. Quest, too, seemed unusually
subdued.

"Better have a trot round and hop over the
practice jump." Sue advised, seeing Sandy's dejected attitude.

In the practice area outside, Sandy cantered
Quest around and then put the chestnut to the
small brush fence. Quest took off too close to the
jump, and they cleared the brush fence awkwardly
and untidily, with Quest's near hind knocking the
fence and Sandy losing a stirrup.

"That was hopeless," Sandy muttered, conscious
of Mrs Marran watching her. "Let's do it again," she
whispered, leaning forward to speak to Quest, who

flicked back her ears to listen. Sandy smoothed the chestnut neck. "Come on, girlie," she said, turning back towards the jump. This time they jumped it easily, and Quest even gave a small buck of pleasure. All of a sudden, Sandy felt wide awake – and excited.

"Good luck!" called a voice, as Sandy and Quest left the practice area. Looking across, Sandy saw Andrea on Rags, standing by the fencing. She had forgotten all about Andrea! Sandy reined in her pony.

"Thanks," she said, "I need it!"

"I'm sure you'll be all right," Andrea said. "Quest looks . . . sort of *confident*."

Andrea was right, Sandy thought, as she trotted the chestnut mare over towards the indoor school; perhaps *too* confident! Quest bounced along, snorting, with her nose pushed up in the air.

Inside the school, Sandy was just in time to see the dark-haired girl from Lollington Stacey complete a faultless round, despite her erratic riding. She trotted her pony out of the ring, her face clouded with temper.

"This stupid animal!" she complained to her friend, jerking at the bay pony's reins irritatedly. "She went right out wide before the wall. We could have knocked off three seconds if we'd cut off the corner."

"Well, you're in charge," pointed out her fellow competitor.

"Oh, *she* thinks she knows best," the dark-haired girl retorted, jerking again on the reins, just for good measure.

"I'm sure she does," Sandy muttered to Adam, who was next to her on Jasper.

"I hate the way she treats that pony," said Adam angrily. "I wish it would stop being so well-behaved and throw her – *I* would!"

Sandy giggled. "You vicious little pony!" she laughed.

Adam blushed. "I don't like seeing a lovely pony being treated like that," he admitted. "She just doesn't know how lucky she is," he added wistfully.

The girl's voice floated across to them again. "I'm going to get something better soon," she told her friend languidly.

"Good," muttered Adam, "then perhaps the pony will have a better home. Hey!" he added, turning to Sandy. "It's your turn next!"

Sandy's stomach lurched as her number was called, and she squeezed Quest into a trot. Sandy could tell that the chestnut pony did not want to take a sedate trip round the jumps. She held her on a tight rein, as they cantered round in a circle near the start. Sandy could feel the power beneath her, waiting to be unleashed.

"Steady, girl, *steady*," she murmured, and was rewarded by a flicked-back ear and a loud snort of impatience. "I know, I know, you want to be off," Sandy told her in a soothing voice, "but we mustn't spoil it by going too fast—"

The bell rang, and Sandy headed her pony towards the start and the first jump. She had not intended to let the chestnut mare begin as fast as she did, but Quest was excited. They flew over the first brush fence and Quest gathered speed, thundering across the school and taking the next fence in her stride.

"Steady, steady!" Sandy spoke in a firm voice, and Quest responded, slowing just enough to take the left hand sweep round with enough room before the next jump. With an excited snort, Quest took off and sailed over the spread, with inches to spare. Sandy hardly saw the next two jumps, as she and Quest thundered down the side of the indoor school, leaping the "road closed" and parallel bars with ease.

At this point, Sandy had to work hard to keep Quest under control, as they turned in a wide curve to the left and then sharply to face the wall. It looked very daunting to Sandy, even from Quest's back, but the mare seemed to view it with pleasure! Taking off from her powerful hindquarters, she soared over the jump, then across the arena and over the gate.

A sharp turn to the right and a couple of strides took them to the corner of the school, where Sandy turned the pony to face the imposing double, followed by a spread. But Quest was not intimidated. She negotiated the double with ease, galloping down the side of the arena to sail over the spread and gallop past the finishing line.

They had circled halfway round the school to loud applause before Sandy was able to bring the pony's speed down to a canter. Sue was at the exit.

"I think you've done it!" she exclaimed, her eyes shining. "We're ahead of Turton Bridge now – and only just behind Lollington Stacey!"

Sandy jumped down from the saddle and put her arms round the chestnut pony. "You clever girl," she said, hugging the mare's sweating neck.

"And she didn't buck once!" Tessa declared, as she and the others gathered round.

After a short break while the jumps were raised, the competitors began again. Tessa and Sandy were able to relax for the moment, since their turns would be after the lunch break. However, the rest of the team members were on edge, with a mixture of excitement and grim determination.

Chrissy's second round brought another fast clear round, and wild clapping from the Heronsway team watching from outside the indoor school. But Lollington Stacey, too, had achieved a second clear round.

"I can't bear it!" Tessa said, nibbling desperately at her now non-existent nails.

The next competitor for Lollington Stacey had a second clear round, but Turton Bridge received eight penalty points for knocked fences. Soon, it was Sue's turn. Her team watched her jump her round anxiously.

"Steady, Beauty, watch that wall!" Chrissy murmured, watching the dun pony apprehensively. But Beauty cleared the wall and the rest of the jumps, finishing the round without faults.

By lunch time, all nerves were taut, and no one ate with much enthusiasm. It was a cold, overcast day, so the Heronsway team took its lunch break in one of the boxes. Adam sat disconsolately, leaning against the side of the van.

"Don't look so miserable, Adam," said Sandy,

looking at him sympathetically. Sarah and Puffin had again cleared all the jumps, but although Adam and Jasper had jumped a fast second round, they had incurred four penalty points.

"But it was so stupid," Adam said crossly. "The 'road closed' was probably the lowest jump there!"

"Jasper only just touched it," Tessa said, offering him a crisp from her packet. "You were just unlucky that it fell."

"And it *was* a very fast round."

Everyone was surprised to hear Andrea's voice joining in the conversation. She had remained very quiet all day.

"That's right," agreed Sarah, "and, anyway, it didn't matter because Lollington Stacey had a refusal."

"But that's only three marks off," Adam reminded her.

"Stop it, all of you!" Sue chided from the cab, where she was eating her packed lunch with Peter. "As long as we're all enjoying ourselves, that's all that matters. I'm enjoying myself. Are you enjoying yourselves?"

"Yes, Sue," they all chorused, obediently. And then they began to laugh.

"We sound so well-behaved!" giggled Sandy.

"Like six-year-olds on a school outing!" Tessa doubled up and began to shake with laughter.

It was infectious. Soon the horse box was rocking, as the six of them rolled around in the straw, helpless with laughter.

Sue peered through at them. "That's better," she said to Peter. "They're more normal now."

118

As shrieks of laughter floated out from the Heronsway horse box, the dark girl from Lollington Stacey passed by. She stopped and looked in at them disbelievingly before moving on.

As Tessa cleared the last jump and gave Duskie a free rein to finish the course as fast as he could, a loud cheer arose from outside the window.

"Well done, Tess!" Sandy shrieked, jumping up and down in the saddle with excitement.

Turton Bridge had had three refusals and had fallen right back, allowing Ludleigh into third place. Still, Lollington Stacey was in the lead, but only just!

"It's up to us, now, girlie," Sandy told the chestnut mare, leaning forward to whisper into Quest's ear. But first the other eight riders would take their turn. Sandy watched apprehensively as the rider for Ludleigh circled round the arena, and then began the course. The pony was strong and nimble, and completed the course without faults. The next competitor had three faults for a refusal, and the next crashed into the wall, having turned the corner too fast. Then it was the turn of the dark-haired girl from Lollington Stacey. She circled her pony round the arena, looking determined, and when the bell rang they began.

"That's going to be a fast round," Sue muttered, as girl and pony flew over the jumps. But this time, when they had cleared the parallel bars, the girl forced her pony to turn left almost immediately, giving it hardly any room before the wall. The bay pony tried to take off, but it was hopeless. At the last moment it refused, crashing into the wall and knocking bricks everywhere.

The dark-haired girl was plainly furious. Yanking her pony round, she whacked it sharply with her crop, before taking it to the corner of the school to wait while the wall was re-built.

Adam was quivering with rage. "I wish she'd fallen off," he muttered.

"Well, at least she's got three faults," Sandy reminded him.

At the next attempt, with more room in which to manoeuvre, the bay pony cleared the wall and then went on to finish the course without further faults. Two more competitors completed their turns, and then Sandy found herself again in the jumping area, with calls of "Good luck!" from the others following her into the arena.

"We mustn't go wrong, Questie, we *mustn't*," Sandy told the pony, and was surprised to hear her own voice quavering with nerves. She cantered round the arena, trying to stop her hands from trembling. She mustn't pass on her nervousness to Quest, she reminded herself.

As they cantered past where Sandy knew the rest of the team would be, she looked over. It was Andrea who caught her eye and called out, "Good luck, Sandy!"

The bell rang, and Sandy's hands tightened on the reins. She felt Quest give a small buck.

"Come on then, Quest, let's go!"

With a new determination, girl and pony headed for the first jump, clearing it easily and heading across the arena towards the next. Again and again, Quest leapt, clearing each jump with ease, and snorting excitedly as she landed. As they flew over the spread, Sandy realized with relief that they had finished without incurring any faults.

"*Good* girl," she said, easing Quest back to a canter when they had passed the finishing line, "You're a clever girl," she added, leaning forward to pat the chestnut enthusiastically. Quest celebrated by bucking again, this time dislodging Sandy from the saddle on to the pony's neck.

The rest of the Heronsway team had gathered by the exit.

"We've done it! We've done it!" The normally quiet Sarah was dancing up and down, shrieking with excitement.

"What have we done? What's the score?" asked Sandy, wriggling back into the saddle, just as the announcement came over the loudspeaker system.

"And that very fast round, without faults, for Heronsway, brings their total points so far in this three day event exactly level with Lollington Stacey. We have a very interesting competition now, ladies and gentlemen, with Ludleigh only five points behind in third place. In two weeks' time, the third and last phase of this competition – the cross-country – will take place at Lollington Stacey, who will be competing on their home ground – so it looks like being an exciting finish!"

14

Perhaps if Sandy had known, she would not have felt so happy on the Saturday evening before the final day of the competition. Life seemed to be going so well. Miss Townsend was pleased with her, Mum was happy, Sue was excited about the competition and the training had been going well. In fact, life seemed to be wonderful!

"Which only goes to show," Sandy was to say miserably to Tessa on the following day, "that you can never be sure of anything."

On Saturday evening, however, Sandy's spirits were high, as she spread clean straw over Quest's well-brushed stable floor. She hummed to herself as she filled the haynet and hung it up.

"You sound cheerful!" It was Tessa who had stopped at the door to speak. She lowered her voice, "And, talking of being more cheerful," she added, "have you noticed Andrea?"

"What do you mean, *noticed*?" Sandy replied innocently.

"She's more ..." Tessa paused, searching for the right word, "human!" she said at last. "Her mother hasn't been around for ages. And you *must* have seen that her riding's improved."

"She does seem to really like jumping," Sandy pointed out.

"And I'm bound to admit that she and Rags are pretty good at it, too," Tessa agreed. "It seems to me," she added, picking up her bucket, "that she's a reformed character. I don't know what's done it, but I'm glad."

As Tessa continued on her way to the stable, with the bucket of food which Duskie was eagerly awaiting, Sandy continued to hum to herself. Yes, life didn't seem so bad. The Andrea problem seemed to have improved since that Saturday night. Now, it was just the parent problem; and Sandy was hoping to be able to do something about that tomorrow. Not only had she persuaded both her parents to come to the cross-country at Lollington Stacey, but also Mum had employed someone to look after the shop for the morning. Dad was picking Mum up, and they were travelling together.

Sandy fetched Quest from the exercising area and led her to her stable. "I'm really looking forward to tomorrow," Sandy told the chestnut pony, and Quest pushed her nose affectionately against Sandy's arm.

Sandy slept well that night and awoke in the early morning with an excited knot in the pit of her stomach. Tessa confessed to the same feeling when they met at the centre.

"I half hoped to wake up with measles or chicken-pox, or something," Tessa admitted. "You know, all covered in spots and Mum saying 'You can't possibly go!' "

"Mm. I know what you mean. Then we could leave it to Andrea!"

As they spoke, Andrea cycled into the yard.

"Hi, Andy!" Tessa called, waving. Sandy looked at her friend in surprise. This was a change of attitude for Tessa!

"She's not so bad when you get to know her," Tessa explained a little sheepishly. "She can't help her parents, can she?"

Sandy smiled to herself as she set about grooming Quest's already shining coat.

There was the usual bustle of preparation, with last-minute changes of headbands, and lost gloves, but at last they were all packed into the two vehicles. The sky was clear, promising a sunny day, and by the time the Heronsway contingent had reached Lollington Stacey, all members of the team – two and four-legged – were hot and sticky.

"Phew, it's warm," Adam said, wiping his hand across his face.

"A real June day," Sue said. She turned to Chrissy, who was leading Merlin down the ramp. "Try and have a gentle warm-up in the shade," she suggested, "since you'll be first round the course for Heronsway. Perhaps we'd all better walk the course," she added. "We've studied the plan, but the real thing might seem a bit different!"

They tramped round the three fields, following the plan.

"It's a big course," Chrissy said.

"Mm. A bit bigger than ours," Sue admitted.

"The jumps are about the same," said Adam, trying to sound more confident than he felt.

"They look enormous," wailed Sarah, "and solid!"

"They're just like ours," Sue said, firmly. "The important thing is to get the course well and truly into your head. Then you won't waste time looking for the next jump. We'll go round again, shall we?"

"I think I know it," said Chrissy, "I'm off to warm up now. I'll be going round it in about three quarters of an hour!"

The rest of the team jogged round the course again and then gathered together by the two Heronsway vehicles, where the ponies were tied up in the shade.

It was just as the loudspeaker announced the beginning of the event, with the first competitor for Turton Bridge, that Chrissy appeared from the field. Her jodhpurs were muddy and she was leading Merlin, who was limping painfully.

"I'm sorry, Sue," Chrissy said dejectedly. "I don't know how it happened. There must have been a hole in the ground. The grass is long in that field. I was just giving him a little canter . . ." Her voice faded miserably.

Sue bent down, feeling Merlin's leg. She straightened up. "You can't help it, Chrissy," she consoled. Then, turning to Adam, she asked, "I don't suppose your dad's here is he?"

"Yes, he's having a day off. He said he'd be here early. I'll go and look, shall I?"

"Yes please, Adam." Sue patted Merlin and looked back at Chrissy. "It's swelling up already," she told her. "I don't think you'll be able to compete."

Adam arrived, dragging his father by the arm.

"A casualty before you start!" said Mr Maiyer. "That's a shame." He was a tall man, with a serious, kind face. He bent to feel the leg carefully, and then stood up again. "I'm sorry," he said, shaking his head. "Plenty of rest for that leg for at least a month, I'm afraid. Certainly no cross-country!"

"It's nearly time for my turn," said Chrissy anxiously.

Sue turned round. "How about it, then?" she said. "Here's your chance, Andrea!"

"But—" Andrea began. Tessa interrupted her.

"No time for buts, Andy," she told her. "You can do it. You and Rags are good at cross-country."

"You've been jumping really well at the practices," Sandy reminded her.

"You *must* do it," said Sarah, "*Please*, Andrea!"

Andrea looked round at them all. "If you really want me to . . ."

"Come on, then," said Sue, holding Ragamuffin's reins while Andrea mounted, "There's no time to lose." She pointed across to the other side of the equestrian centre. "Over to the edge of that field and wait for your number to be called. Ponies and riders go in threes to that little collecting ring by the first jump and they'll tell you there when to start. Oh! I nearly forgot!" She turned to Chrissy and quickly unpinned the number from her shirt. "Bend down," she instructed Andrea, "and I'll put this on for you. Then I'll go and tell the organisers. You're number fifty-eight."

"Good luck, Andrea!"

"You can do it, Andy!"

To a chorus of good wishes, Andrea and Raga-muffin trotted away towards the first field.

"I'm just going to see if I can find Mum and Dad," Sandy told Tessa. "Where shall we stand to see Andrea?"

"How about the bank?" Tessa suggested. "That's number nine on the course. It looks horrible! I want to see how other people cope with it."

"OK. See you in ten minutes."

Sandy made for the car park. Her eyes searched the spectators who were arriving. Most of them seemed to be settling by the fences close to jump number ten. Sandy located her mother, who appeared to be deep in conversation with Adam's father. Just as she had seen Dad, who was wandering round the stables looking at the ponies, she heard her name being called.

"Oh, Sandy, there you are!" It was Kay, who hurried over to her. "I'm glad I found you."

"How are you?" Sandy asked. Kay had not been to Heronsway for several weeks.

"Oh, I'm fine, thanks – so far." She smiled. "I'm keeping my fingers crossed, this time." She looked serious as she spoke again. "Sandy, I wanted to speak to you. I don't want to spoil your day, but I feel I must tell you *now*, because I shall be telling other people today – I have to get on with it, I'm afraid."

"What – what about?" Sandy suddenly felt a chill inside her. She could tell that Kay had something awful to tell her, and it *must* concern Quest.

"Sandy." Kay rested a hand on her arm. "You've looked after Quest beautifully, and I've really

127

appreciated it, but ... I've thought about it a lot and I really can't afford to go on keeping her at livery – even do-it-yourself, which is cheaper than full livery."

"So – so, what—" Sandy stammered, finding herself unable to speak in full sentences.

"I don't want to sell her – at least I don't think so," Kay explained. "I can't ride her just now, and I don't want to risk anything happening to the baby, so I wouldn't ride her until after the birth. And then I probably shan't be able to ride for a while, so ... so I've decided to let her go on temporary loan for a year."

"Oh ... I see." The chill that Sandy felt inside spread to the whole of her body. "So she might not stay at Heronsway?"

"Probably not. I'm going to mention it to Mrs Marran from Ludleigh. She tried to buy Quest from me after the dressage competition. I've told Sue, but she doesn't want to take on any more ponies just now. I'm terribly sorry, Sandy."

"You can't help it," Sandy replied, miserably. "It's a good idea – I can see that. I only wish I could have her, but ..." That was a hopeless thought, Sandy knew. Mum worked hard at the shop, but she was busy working up the business, so there was very little money to spare just now.

In a dejected daze, Sandy wandered back to jump number nine, where she was meeting Tessa. She had forgotten about seeing Mum and Dad.

"Hi!" Tessa greeted her, cheerfully. "Did you find them?"

"Who?"

"Your parents, dope!" Tessa looked at her closely. "You OK?" she asked, "You look as if you've seen a ghost, or something."

Miserably, Sandy told her what Kay had said.

"That's awful!" Tessa agreed. "But perhaps someone else will want their pony looked after," she pointed out helpfully. "We'll look on the notice board when we get back. And I'll share Duskie with you," she added, generously.

"Thanks, Tess." Sandy sat down hard on the long grass under the hedge. "But it won't be Quest, will it?" she said, dejectedly.

"Oh come on, cheer up," said practical Tessa. "Something will turn up. Look!" she added, "Andrea's started. She's going quite fast!"

Sandy spent the rest of the morning with Quest. She had lost interest in the competition. While Quest pulled at the grass, Sandy leaned against the hedge and talked to the chestnut pony.

"I'm sure Mrs Marran will look after you," Sandy told her favourite pony. "Maybe Dad will treat me to a ride sometimes, like he tried to before," she added, cheering up a little at this thought. "I can ask for you then, can't I?" She stroked the pale chestnut nose, and Quest stopped munching to peer at her curiously. Then, snorting contentedly into the long grass, the pony started eating again.

Sandy could hear the loudspeaker in the distance, and sometimes she heard Heronsway mentioned. She could hear the sound of voices, and the thud of hooves as each competitor passed by in the next field.

129

"You're not much company today," Tessa grumbled, when she arrived with the others at the lunch time break.

Andrea sat down next to Sandy. "I'm so sorry," she murmured, "Tessa's just told me."

Adam bounded up, his normally pale and serious face flushed with heat and excitement.

"Did you have a good round?" Sandy asked him, remembering guiltily that she was part of a team.

"Not bad," Adam admitted, "but Sarah was better. And Andrea was fantastic!" He sat down on the other side of her. "But your mum has been the best of all!" he stated emphatically.

Sandy sat up and stared at him. "You're not going to tell me that Mum rode Beauty instead of Sue!" she exclaimed.

"Of course not, idiot!" Adam said. "Sue had a really fast round. Your mum," he continued, "has persuaded Dad that I shouldn't go to the grammar school! She was standing next to him, you see, and they got talking, apparently, and when she knew who he was she started telling him how much better off I'd be at the comp!"

"Mm. She's quite persuasive sometimes," Sandy agreed.

"She's fantastic!" said Adam. "But that's not all!"

"What then?"

"Well, when I'd finished my go, I went and stood by Dad, and he seemed quite . . . pleased about my ride round the course." Adam pushed at his straight brown hair excitedly. "And then I saw that girl – you know, the one from Lollington Stacey with the lovely bay mare."

"Yes?"

"And I told him about her. He hates bad treatment of animals, you see."

"And when I told him what she said at the last competition," Adam continued, tumbling over his words in his excitement, "you know, about getting something better – do you know what he said?"

"Adam!" Sandy said, exasperated. "How could I?"

"He said – 'Would *you* like that pony?' "

"Wow!" Sandy stared at him. "Did he mean it?"

"Of course he did. He doesn't say things like that unless he means them," Adam stated with conviction.

"Hey! That's great!" exclaimed Sandy, forgetting her misery. "Is he going to buy the pony?"

"Well, the last I saw of him, he was off to find her," Adam replied. "I thought I should come back here to put Jasper in the shade."

"That's great, Adam," Sandy repeated, but this time her voice was flat. "Now you'll all have ponies."

"But you can share Puffin," said Sarah, quickly.

"And I told you I'd share Duskie," Tessa added.

"And Rags," put in Andrea.

"That's right," Adam added. "We're a team, don't forget!"

15

"This might be the last time I ride you, Questie,"
Sandy whispered into the chestnut's ear, which had
flicked back to listen, "but we're going to jump better than we've ever jumped, aren't we, girlie?"

Quest danced sideways, eyeing the pony next to
her. The chestnut pony felt as though she were on
springs. In fact, Sandy thought, she felt like one big
spring!

"Right. Off you go, you three," said the steward,
pointing across the field. "Over there, by that tent.
That's the start – and the finish. Good luck!"

The three ponies trotted across the field, past
two of the jumps. At the tent, near the start, their
names and numbers were noted again, and they
were told to stand in or near a small collecting
ring.

"Don't get in the way of the finishers," the steward warned. "You can trot round a bit to warm up,
over there," she added, pointing beyond the collecting ring, "but stay in the collecting ring when
I call your number, because that means you'll be
next!"

The dark-haired girl from Lollington Stacey had
begun her round just before Sandy and her two
companions had crossed the field. Now, Sandy saw
her coming back across the second field. She and

her pony had just negotiated the bank successfully, and were cantering through the gateway before turning left and heading fast for jump number ten, double poles, which they jumped easily. They cleared the next jump. Then Sandy lost sight of them behind a dip in the field. She imagined them clearing the wall and then making for the water jump. They were nearly at the finish.

Sandy sat dejectedly in the saddle. Heronsway's only hope had been that Lollington Stacey would incur some faults by this, their last competitor. They had crept ahead of the Heronsway team, despite a good round by Tessa, and now Sandy felt dispirited. She and Quest couldn't possibly go fast enough to catch up. The second of her two companions started off on the course, and Sandy was told to wait in the collecting ring.

"Have you warmed up enough?" Sue appeared at her side, looking up anxiously.

"Yes, she's OK," said Sandy, smoothing Quest's fine coat. "But there's no hope of the cup, now, is there?" she added. "I can't do it, Sue."

Sue looked up at her. "Sandy, it doesn't matter about the cup," she said. "But you could do it, you know," she added.

"But they must be well ahead now," Sandy argued.

Sue shook her head. "Lollington's last competitor had six faults for two refusals," she told her.

As Sandy waited for her number to be called, Sue told her briefly of the dark-haired girl's attempt at the water jump. She had brought her pony up from the wall too close to the hedge, trying to save time.

The bay pony had turned sharply and had been faced suddenly with the water jump.

"She would have been all right if that girl had just eased her down to it," Sue said. "After all, the pony must *know* the jump. But you know how that girl rides," Sue continued, scornfully. "She shouted and lashed at her with the crop, and the pony refused. Poor thing was terrified."

Sandy began to show some interest. "And the second time?" she asked incredulously. From what Sandy had seen of the bay pony, she seemed a gentle, well-mannered pony, her main fault being her rider!

"Well, that girl just got the pony in such a lather," Sue said.

"Number one hundred and three," a voice called.

"That's me!" Sandy's stomach lurched.

"Have a go, Sandy," Sue called, "Good luck!"

"Off you go!" shouted the steward.

Taken by surprise, Sandy dug her heels into Quest's sides, and the pony sprang away as if she had been stung.

"Sorry, girlie," Sandy muttered, as they flew over the first small jump, which consisted of a row of tyres joined together. "Steady," she said, reining in as they reached the first gateway. Once through the narrow opening, Sandy gave Quest her head, and they galloped up the side of the next field. Sandy turned her pony when she felt that there was enough room to negotiate the next jump, an innocuous-looking brush fence. She allowed Quest to gather speed, and as they flew over the jump, her mind was thinking ahead.

"Bales of straw next, Quest," she called, above the sound of thundering hooves. Quest took the jump almost contemptuously, leaping the narrow jump between two high hedges.

They galloped down the side of the next field towards jump number four – two logs with about twenty inches between them. From the approach, the jump seemed an easy one, but Sandy knew that it was quite a spread. She slowed her pony's pace a little, so that Quest took off at the right distance from the jump.

"Lovely!" Sandy shouted in Quest's ear, as the chestnut mare soared over the wide logs. As they turned sharply and thundered towards the next jump, Sandy remembered how narrow it was, with high posts on either side and with deceptively wide planks between. She eased on the reins and the pony slowed reluctantly. Quest leapt the jump neatly. The next jump was quite close, to the right, but Sandy galloped Quest on, turning the corner of the field, before heading her towards the jump. The narrow jump negotiated, Sandy gave Quest her head as they galloped across the field towards the ditch. They slowed before the jump, and trotted through a dip, before scrambling up and jumping the low wall. As they turned left, moving fast, Sandy steadied her pony for she knew that they had to cross a metalled lane. A single bar was next, and then jump number nine loomed ahead. "Horrible" was how Tessa had described it, and Sandy was inclined to agree with her. But the others had managed it, Sandy reminded herself. Not too fast and not too slow for this one, she thought.

Viewed from the side, the bank looked very tricky, but from this angle, as she and Quest approached it from the front, Sandy told herself that it didn't look so bad. A long, steep grassy bank led up to a low solid log jump at the top. But Sandy knew that that was not all! She cantered Quest steadily up the slope, jumping her carefully over the log. Straight away, without time for another stride, came another log, which Quest leapt over like a cat. The landing on the other side was on a downward slope. Three strides, down the other side of the bank and then came another solid-looking log jump. Quest leapt, well clear of the log, and with a sigh of relief, Sandy let her have her head for a few strides. She eased her back for the gateway, and turned her to the left. At this stage, Sandy really let Quest have her head. Two fairly low but wide jumps were ahead of them – a spread of two poles, followed by a row of oil drums lying on their sides. Quest galloped down the side of the field. Sandy could feel the pony's excitement flowing through her. As they soared over the poles and then the oil drums, Sandy thought that she had never done anything as exciting in her life as this cross-country. She could hardly contemplate that anyone else was there, except herself and Quest. She was aware of faces and voices and ponies, as she and Quest hurtled on, but all she really knew was that Quest's strong legs were taking them over the jumps and round the fields at a speed faster than she had ever known on the back of a pony. And it was so exciting!

They flew over the barrels and galloped on

towards the gate where they had waited earlier to be sent across to the start. Sandy slowed her pony a little at the corner of the field, and then headed to her right to tackle jump number twelve, a low wall set on an upward slope. Sandy could feel the strength in Quest as the chestnut mare galloped up the slope and surged over the wall. They kept going, galloping up, close to the hedge and then, suddenly, the water jump was there.

"Oh no!" Sandy thought, "I've done the same as the dark-haired girl!" She pulled frantically on the reins to slow her pony as they went down the slope to the water. Quest skidded to a halt at the water's edge, her head thrown up, snorting loudly.

Sandy's heart sank. How could she have been so stupid – now they had had a refusal.

"Come on, girlie," she said, soothingly, freeing the reins and leaning forward. "It's all right. It isn't deep." Almost unseating her, Quest leapt forward without further ado, plunging into the water and galloping up and out at the other side.

Showering water as they went, pony and rider galloped on.

"Only one more difficult jump," Sandy told herself, as they thundered on towards the next jump, an innocuous low pole jump on level ground, halfway down the side of the field.

Sandy hardly noticed the pole jump as Quest took it in her stride. Her mind was racing ahead to the next obstacle, called looping-the-loop in the programme. It was a complicated-looking jump, consisting of fencing formed into an "S" shape, but really, Sandy told herself, it was quite straight-forward. The main requirement was that the pony should be completely controlled, since otherwise a great deal of time could be wasted.

"Easy, girl, easy," Sandy murmured, bringing Quest back to a collected canter. They approach-ed the maze-like jump carefully, passing between fencing to jump the rail ahead of them. As soon as they had landed, Sandy eased Quest to a trot, turned her sharply round to face in the opposite direction, then urged her on to a canter. Quest had time for just two strides, and then was up and over the second rail.

Leaning forward, Sandy turned her pony's head for home and gave her a free rein. They galloped towards the last jump, flying over the pile of logs at speed. Then they were past the finishing line, and Sandy was easing on the reins, gradually bringing the excited chestnut mare back to a canter. At last, Sandy became aware of people near her. Tessa was leaping up and down, shouting something at her. And there were Mum and Dad, standing togeth-er by the fence. As Sandy waved, Quest gave an enormous buck, sending her rider soaring over her head.

Sandy was winded as she landed. She tried to sit up, but she couldn't breathe properly for a moment, so she lay where she was, gasping for air. Then, as the air reached her lungs again, she sat up and saw Mum and Dad hurrying towards her.

A plan instantly leapt into Sandy's mind. If they thought she was hurt, they might realize that they should be together again – that their poor little younger daughter needed *both* parents to look after her! Sandy leaned back again, and groaned realistically.

"Sandy, are you all right?" Mum's face peered anxiously at her.

"What hurts?" asked Dad.

"My . . . er . . . leg." Sandy grabbed her right leg. "Ouch!" she said, and instantly regretted saying it, for her cry didn't sound too convincing!

"But you landed on the other leg," Mum pointed out.

Sue's face appeared above her. "Well done, Sandy – we've won!" she said excitedly, adding, as an afterthought, "You're OK, aren't you?"

"What! We've won the cup? But I had a refusal."

"No, you didn't," Sue replied. "Quest only paused for a moment. She didn't step back."

"Great!" Before she realized what she was doing, Sandy was on her feet, and grabbing the reins of an excited and unrepentant chestnut pony, who had returned to the scene of the crime to see what was keeping her rider!

With all thoughts of pretending to be injured and in need of parental protection swept away, Sandy joined in the general hilarity of the Heronsway team. Mum and Dad smiled at each other and walked away towards the coffee bar.

16

Sandy had avoided Kay all day. After the competition was over, and the cup had been presented to Sue and her team from Heronsway, Sandy had slipped away, under the pretence of taking Quest to the shade near the horseboxes. She didn't want to know. She didn't want to hear how eagerly Mrs Marran had agreed the terms for taking over Quest for the next year. Nor did she want to hear that the horsebox would be calling the next day to pick up the chestnut mare and transport her to Ludleigh. She even imagined that Kay had avoided *her* – not wanting to spoil Sandy's day by telling her the new arrangements after her triumphant finish.

Sandy was quiet during the ride home. Although she joined in Sue's impromptu party, after the ponies had been stabled and fed, she excused herself early and returned to Quest's stable.

"I'll be here in the morning," she promised the pony, "but maybe not in the evening." She bit her lip, forcing back tears that threatened. "But I'll come and see you, Questie, as often as I can." Quest was not paying too much attention. Tired after her long and energetic day, she rested one hind leg and dozed, her eyes closing.

Sandy smoothed the chestnut neck and tickled Quest behind the ears. Then she let herself out of the stable quietly, bolting the door carefully behind her. Near the hay barn she met Tessa, who was also on her way home.

"I'm tired," Tessa said, reinforcing her statement by yawning loudly as she pulled her bicycle from its daytime resting place. She looked across at Sandy. "You've been terribly quiet this afternoon," she stated.

Sandy lifted her bike from the barn. As the girls cycled slowly down the cinder path away from the equestrian centre, Sandy told Tessa her fears.

"The trouble with you," Tessa said bluntly, "is you're too imaginative. I expect Kay will take *ages* to find someone."

"Oh no," Sandy said, with conviction. "I'm sure she's found someone already."

The light was on in the kitchen when Sandy arrived home.

"Hi!" Sandy poked her head round the door to greet her mother. "Dad gone?" she asked.

"Yes." Mum looked up. She had a strange look on her face, Sandy thought – a pleased look. They must have made it up, Sandy decided. She stepped into the kitchen. "I'm starving," she announced, suddenly realizing the fact. "Did you have a good day?" she added.

"Yes thanks, dear."

Mum had an odd sound to her voice, too – excited, almost. It *must* be something to do with her and Dad. Strangely, Sandy herself didn't feel particularly excited about it. She had wanted to get Mum and Dad together again, but over the

141

last weeks and months she had grown used to living with Mum only. Dad had always been away from home a lot, anyway, and when he came to see them now, he didn't stay long. Still, Sandy thought that she should prompt Mum a bit.

"Did Dad . . . *say* anything – leave a message?" she asked.

"Yes, I have got a message for you – but it's from me and Dad."

Sandy cut herself some bread and made a cheese sandwich.

"Dad and I feel that perhaps we haven't been fair to you," Mum continued, pouring Sandy a mug of tea. "And after today, we feel we ought to explain to you properly." Mum sighed. "But you know what Dad's like. He never stays long enough – always has to rush off somewhere. So he left it to me." Mum grinned across the table at her daughter. "We know what you were up to today, you know," she said, laughing.

Sandy, her mouth full of cheese sandwich, opened her eyes to look suitably innocent.

"You've been trying to get us together again, haven't you?" Mum continued, her eyes twinkling. "Getting Dad to look at my kitchen cupboards and bringing us together at your riding events." She laughed out loud. "And faking an injured leg today so that we'd feel you needed us both around!"

Suddenly she was serious again. "Well, Dad and I have talked, and we feel we should have explained before now. We're still good friends, you see, Sandy, but—" Mum stopped to stroke Boxer, who had jumped up on to her knee.

"Well, we're not the same people that we were twenty years ago, when we got married. And now we don't want the same kind of life. Dad is ambitious and loves living in the city and – oh, all the things I don't like. So we've decided . . ." She looked across at Sandy anxiously, "to stay good friends but to get divorced, because we each want a completely different kind of life. Do you understand, Sandy?"

Sandy nodded as she swallowed the last mouthful of her sandwich. "I think so, Mum. I think I was beginning to realize, anyway. Dad's always on the move, always rushing around, isn't he? But we . . ." Sandy did not finish her sentence, but Mum understood, and smiled across at her.

"Dad has been offered a marvellous job," Mum went on, leaning forward. "He'll have a flat in London, but he'll be travelling all over Europe – just the kind of thing he loves. He wants you to know that you can go up to London and stay with him, when he's there—"

"If I can catch him at home!" Sandy interrupted, and they both laughed. Sandy was glad that Mum had spoken about it and explained.

Mum's secretly excited look came back as she spoke again.

"Oh – and I've got another message for you," she said, casually.

"From Dad?"

"No – from Kay."

Sandy's happy mood evaporated. So she *had* been right. Kay had found a home for Quest.

"Oh." Sandy's voice was hardly audible.

"She said she'll see you tomorrow with all Quest's details."

"Wh – what?" Sandy looked bewildered. Mum was smiling, and her secretly pleased look had come out into the open.

"It's Dad, you see," Mum explained. "This new job means a lot more money, and he wants us to benefit, too. And when Andrea told me about—"

"Andrea!" Sandy was getting more confused every minute.

"Yes. Someone told her I was your mother and she came over. She told me how much you love Quest and about Quest needing a temporary home and about Mrs Marran at Ludleigh. And Dad was there, you see, and we talked about it and—" Mum stopped for a moment to smile again at Sandy. "Dad went over to see Kay and arranged for *you* to have Quest. She'll be your own pony for the next year!"

It was all very confusing, Sandy decided, as she drifted off to sleep. But what did it matter *how* it had happened? The important thing was that Quest was to be hers for a whole year.

As sleep took a firmer hold on her, Sandy's thoughts dwelled on the beautiful chestnut mare, with her intelligent dark eyes and her long, silky forelock. Tomorrow, she would see Quest, groom her, talk to her. Tomorrow she would gallop her along the tracks on the moors. Tomorrow . . . tomorrow . . .